the bluebird café

the bluebird café

rebecca smith

BLOOMSBURY

First published in Great Britain 2001

Bloomsbury Publishing Plc, 38 Soho Square, London W1D 3HB

A CIP catalogue record is
available from the British Library

ISBN 0 7475 5332 7

10 9 8 7 6 5 4 3 2 1

Typeset by Hewer Text Ltd, Edinburgh
Printed in Great Britain by Clays Limited, St Ives plc

To Stephen

PROLOGUE

'Don't hurt her. She's a pet,' Gilbert's soft Hampshire voice implored.

Hurting the blue budgie was what Lucy feared, what put her in such a flap. She was balanced on a wobbly stool with a Badger Centre tea towel, not quite able to reach the bird. It was now perched on the rods of a mobile. Her friend Abigail was beside her on a table with a colander and a menu.

'Don't hurt her. She's a pet.'

It was a brand-new budgie. An impulse buy. Gilbert had wanted to show it to them, had opened the slim white box just a fraction. Lucy had wondered if it was kind to be transporting a bird in something the size of a pencil case. How those folded wings must have been straining against the thin card.

'Don't hurt her. She's a pet. She's for a present.'

Abigail handed Lucy a tablecloth. Where the hell was Paul with his bird-holding skills when they needed him most? A customer came in and the budgie flew into another corner.

Paul was on the Common, sitting under a tree, with his favourite book, *The Illustrated Natural History of Selborne* by Gilbert White, a Gilbert who was wholly unconnected in Paul's mind to the Gilbert back home in the café. He read the 'Advertisement' at the front of the book with undiminished pleasure.

1

The Author of the following Letters takes the liberty, with all proper deference, of laying before the public his idea of *parochial history*, which, he thinks, ought to consist of natural productions and occurances as well as antiquities. He is also of opinion that if stationary men would pay some attention to the districts on which they reside, and would publish their thoughts respecting the objects that surround them, from such materials might be drawn the most complete county-histories, which are still wanting in several parts of this kingdom, and in particular in the county of *Southampton* . . .

Gil. White
Selborne
1 January 1788.

1

John Vir pulled up the metal shutters. It was a moment that he dreaded, another day. He glanced down the empty road to confirm that the paperboys were, as usual, nowhere in sight. John was not his real name. He was called Jagdish, but everyone, all his customers, called him John. A thick tick book that dated back many years showed that he was everyone's friend. The shop was called 'Vir and Vir – News and Food'. The other Vir was his brother who only put in an appearance when his family's food stocks got very low and Iceland was closed.

John Vir might have described himself as separated, but he was still married. His wife Pali had been visiting her family in India for the last five years. He imagined her drinking cups of tea and eating mangoes in the sun. The mangoes in the shop were turning mushy, and her abandoned tin of Tibet sandalwood talc was rusting in the bathroom cabinet. He couldn't bring himself to throw it away.

How beautiful she'd been when they'd met, a month before the wedding, so graceful, like a gazelle. But marriage, Southampton and the shop hadn't suited her. The customers annoyed her, their two sons and a daughter, Gurpal, grew up unruly, and her back ached from sitting behind the till. When she'd gone to visit her parents she'd bought a single ticket.

'In the long run it will be cheaper,' she said. And she had, as usual, been right.

Even now, five years later, there were still things in the shop that had outstayed her. Some celery soups had petrified in their packets and there was stuff at the bottom of the freezer . . .

He sold everything from *Gay Times* to *The Lady*; *Marxism Today*, *Caribbean Times*, the *Irish Post*, the *Daily Telegraph*.

'We have every spice under the sun,' John Vir told his customers. 'Just ask me.' Boxes of fruit studded with dew and drosophila, and vegetables in their prime and past it were in crates on newspaper at the head of the central aisle. Tampax were stacked next to boxes of henna for celebration Mendi hand-painting; all life was there. At the very back of the shop was a silver door to a private chamber. Dead creatures hung inside. When John Vir opened the door an icy wind gusted into the shop. There was speculation that Mrs Vir was spending her holiday inside that cupboard.

Vir and Vir was the only shop that still stocked Spacedust. John didn't want to clear things out. Most of the time he didn't notice, and when something with SELL BY NOVEMBER 86 did catch his eye he thought that perhaps it might be valuable, perhaps a collector or a film company might want it, perhaps his descendants could sell it when 2086 came around.

Gurpal and her brothers were meant to help him in the shop. They were also meant to be at school. When they 'helped out' they sat behind the counter and talked to their friends on the phone. The boys helped themselves to money from the till. Gurpal was addicted to pistachios, Magnums, Feasts, samosas and packets of crisps. John had a recurring dream of the shop melting into a pool of Patak's Curry Paste and cruddy milk, and floating away down the gutter.

Despite the erratic staffing Vir and Vir did OK. He was patronised by students who bought endless copies of the

Independent and lived on Mighty White bread, Hula Hoops, Diet Coke and Sunny Delight. He had hundreds of Asian customers, and people came from all over the city, especially on Sundays, to buy chicken legs, coriander, spices and huge sacks of rice, lentils and flour. He had a licence to sell alcohol and wondered about videos.

Lucy and Paul were favoured customers. They filled their basket with okra and spinach, they experimented with spices and had only occasional lapses into Snickers and Dr Pepper. Lucy bought crazy things: catnip mice, pots of glitter, hair bobbles, spangly combs, candles, Lucky bags, out-of-season Diwali cards. When John went to the Cash and Carry he thought of her.

Lucy didn't hear John Vir open his metal shutters. She woke when Fennel jumped on to the bed and started to fight her feet. She twitched her toes in provocation and opened her eyes. The first thing she saw was Paul's pale neck. He had the very white skin of the red-haired. There were freckles on his shoulders; Lucy liked these, they reminded her of bananas, but he had a stubborn three-week-old spot on one of his top vertebrae. When they made love she had to try not to touch it. Lucy wished that she was in Italy. Somewhere, anywhere warmer, somewhere by the proper sea.

Every morning Lucy went to Vir and Vir to buy a paper, milk and other boring things. When she'd first seen John Vir she'd thought that he looked like Robert De Niro, but that was before she'd seen many films with Joe Mantegna in. The shop opened at 7.30, but at 8.30 Lucy would be one of the first customers. She usually arrived while a man in a white cotton hat was lining up trays of fresh samosas. If she was late she'd be caught in a crowd of schoolchildren buying penny sweets, 5p bags of corn snacks, and plastic tubs of traffic-light-coloured drinks. 'Think of the Es!' Lucy thought, as she resisted the temptation to kick a shover, or give a shiny, pink-ribboned plait a surreptitious tug.

Lucy tried to have the right money ready. If John Vir was busy at the back of the shop or with a delivery, she'd leave it on the counter and shout: 'It's by the till!' Sometimes he didn't turn around, sometimes he did.

2

The Bluebird Café occupied premises that had once belonged to Snookes Electrical Stores. Lucy, Paul and Abigail had viewed the place just before it closed down. Mr Snooke had made a sign on brown cardboard saying SAIL in watery blue letters, but no more customers came. The shelves remained thinly stocked with dusty headphones and kettles. Mice had chewed their way through out-of-date sound systems in the stockroom, and made a luxurious home in the box of the solitary juice extractor. At the back of the shop was Mr Snooke's workshop where, in happier times, he'd made his living by repairing Dansettes and hairdryers for students. The students who came to Southampton now brought huge systems with five years' extended warranty. They threw away anything broken. Lucy thought the place was ideal and bought a device for heating one mug of water.

'Exactly right,' she said, and nobody knew whether she meant the shop or the gadget. Mr Snooke turned away. He didn't hear them leave, he'd not got around to fixing the bell. They didn't go back until Mr Snooke had gone.

Lucy and Paul moved into the flat above the shop, and with a Regeneration Budget grant from the council, they began the make-over. They took down Mr Snooke's metal shelves and painted the walls the colour of Greek yoghurt. Abigail and Lucy stencilled blue doves below the picture rail and bought stripped pine chairs from the Oxfam furniture store. £5 each. The stockroom became a kitchen with two stoves, two sinks, a freezer and a big American fridge which they called the Chiller. Lucy made a noticeboard from wood, green felt and string. Local craftspeople were invited to enquire within about exhibiting their wares. They bought a fridge counter so that people could see the salads and puddings (segregated), and a hot counter too. They bought tables, plates, cutlery, recycled napkins, glasses, the whole IKEA kitchen experience in spades. They put ads in the local papers, and made a banner for the window saying: THE BLUEBIRD CAFE – OPENING MAY 10. Finally, they went to a wholefood co-op for supplies of food and large quantities of a compound that repelled but didn't endanger the lives of mice.

'I hope you appreciate all the help Abigail's giving you,' said Teague, who was Abigail's boyfriend. 'We are meant to be finishing our PhDs, you know.'

'So's Paul,' said Lucy. But Paul spent most of his time at Southampton Common. He was a volunteer at the Badger Centre. The subject of his PhD was 'Climatic Change and Prickle Density Variation in Urban Hedgehogs', but he spent most of his time bird-watching and clearing out the Small Native Mammals.

The café opened on time. It was not a great success. The press stayed away, and most of the tables remained empty. Some students came but ate conservatively. An apple pudding turned brown and had to be whisked out of sight. A tape of the Corrs went down best, and Lucy added Crap Music to her mental shopping list. Just before closing time their Small Business Adviser showed up. Lucy didn't recognise him at first, but Paul did.

'Mr Pillory! Good of you to come,' he said heartily.

'Call me Frank,' he told them for the tenth time.

'But are you?' said Lucy. He was known to them as Frank the Bank.

He brushed some white specks from his shoulders on to the table. Lucy felt her lips drag themselves across her teeth into a smile.

'Sit down. Please have some food,' she said.

Frank Pillory wondered what such a pretty girl was doing mixed up in a risky, low-profit venture like this hippie café. If only he could offer her something at the bank, but those days were gone. There was no certainty any more.

'How's trade?' he asked.

'Oh, booming, booming!' boomed Paul.

'What would you like to eat?' asked Lucy. 'There's carrot cake, coconut cake, cherry flapjacks, coffee, twenty-something types of tea . . .'

He looked at the blackboard.

'I'll try the soup first.'

'Coming right up!' said Lucy, attempting jauntiness.

'And then perhaps . . .'

'Coffee?' Paul suggested.

'The watercress quiche, five-bean pasta salad and a white roll.'

'We offer butter or a non-dairy alternative,' Lucy told him.

'Oh.'

Paul remembered being very small and climbing the steps of the travelling library each week for months to renew *The Tiger Who Came to Tea*. He must tell Lucy to put Tiger Food on her list in case a tiger should come to tea and eat everything they had. Frank Pillory tucked into his carrot soup. It tasted faintly of mud. The quiche was on the table and getting cold before the soup was finished. He left his bowl half full.

'Very nice, tomato was it?'

'Carrot, but with tomato,' said Lucy, politely.

'I must tell my brother about you. He could bring his kids.'

'We do hope to attract families,' said Lucy, who didn't. She could hear some students talking about whether or not they agreed with the conspiracy theorists about the lunar non-landings. The café had a long way to go before it became the haven for artists and intellectuals that she had planned. At least her copy of Françoise Sagan's *Bonjour Tristesse* was there, steadying a wobbling table.

'And at least,' she told Paul, in bed that night, 'Frank the Bank will spend tomorrow in agonies of flatulence.'

'Hmm?'

'He had thirds of five-bean pasta salad.'

Five-bean pasta salad certainly wasn't on the menu at Armando's, Lucy's favourite restaurant, the night the Bluebird, a joint venture of friends, headed by Lucy, had been conceived. Armando's was Southampton's finest Italian restaurant. It was decorated in the traditional style, green, red and white, with plastic and real lobsters and bunches of grapes, and crazy pictures of fountains.

Lucy and Paul, Abigail and Teague, all in their mid-twenties, were admitting to surprise and misgivings at still being in Southampton three years after they'd graduated from the university. While the other three were worthily occupied with PhDs, Lucy was floundering. She had been the restaurant critic of the local free listings magazine (unpaid), but it had just folded, bankrupt. She wanted to leave her job as admin worker at Southampton Kids' Clubs Association. The Kids got on her nerves.

There were people dancing. A fiftieth birthday party with women in strappy, some backless, dresses and lots of jewellery.

'Promise to tell me if I ever get a fat back,' said Abigail, audibly, Lucy feared.

Abigail's five-foot nine-inch frame was as slim and smooth as one of the many clay pipe stems she dug up each week. Her dark blonde hair was precision cut; she was very vain about it. She had small, often muddy paws. Lucy thought that she always looked fantastic, especially in her digging clothes. Abigail and Teague had been the golden couple of the Archaeology Department, but then the opposition hadn't been that hot.

Lucy and Abigail had met on their first day at the university. They shared a kitchen, as well as the cultural heritage of Surrey girls, and were soon united against the Christian wets and engineers who dominated their corridor.

When the waiter took Lucy's coat he said: 'Oh, Sophia Loren!'

This was stretching it a bit. Lucy had dark hair and looked sallow in winter. She was wearing a light green shift dress. She wondered if he meant she looked buxom. She'd always wanted to look like Katharine Hepburn.

But the food was delicious.

'You could do this, Lucy, just as well,' Paul said. Spaghetti Arrabiata was one of his favourites. 'Mmm.' Hot food made him flush red.

'The thermal effect of eating,' said Teague, 'excessive in Paul's case. Studies have been done on it.'

'If I'm not going to be a film star,' mused Lucy, 'I have always wanted to open a café.'

'You should. I'll help,' said Abigail.

'OK. I might just try.'

The waiters had come in banging saucepan lids together and singing 'Happy Birthday' to one of the fat-backed women. It seemed a fitting start. As a future restaurateur, Lucy should have noticed the sneers and the sighs of the staff as they retreated to the kitchen to cut up the cake.

3

The Wayside Hotel was the cheapest in Southampton and Gilbert lived there. It had special rates for the unemployed, but the stony face of the proprietor belied the poster, faded marker pen on green fluorescent card, DSS WELCOME. Once Gilbert had proved his eligibility for housing benefit he had been allowed to drag his tartan trolley up the three flights of stairs to his new home. He was almost forty and he had nothing else.

In his room was a sink with a mirror tile and a shaving point, a double bed with the inevitable orange candlewick cover, a wardrobe with chained-in coat hangers, a lukewarm radiator, and a bedside cabinet sort of thing where he kept his books – *What to Look for in Autumn*, *Keeping Finches*, *Parrots as Pets* and the *Observer's Book of British Birds*. No pets were allowed at the Wayside, but in the room next door a young woman kept tame rats and a baby slept in a drawer.

Downstairs was a TV lounge where residents gathered in the evenings. *Strike It Rich* was very popular, and petty criminals united to see *Crimewatch* and *The Bill*. When *Who Wants to Be a Millionaire?* was on they all shouted out the answers and groaned.

You could easily tell the workers from the unemployed. Almost all of them did shifts at the Kipling's factory. They rose at odd hours and wore white overalls dusted with icing sugar. They gave cakes to their friends, and Gilbert's diet was sometimes supplemented by rejected Fondant Fancies and Mini Bakewells.

It was Saturday, so Gilbert was wearing his corduroy jacket. It stretched across his pudgy back and flapped like a skirt around his thighs. It was the colour of Caramac, and the smartest thing he had. He ate with care and hardly spilled anything on its generous lapels. He cleaned his teeth, J-clothed his shoes and left, sliding downhill on rotten leaves to the bus stop. Behind him another chunk of stucco fell off the Wayside Hotel.

Gilbert didn't often catch the bus into town. He could easily walk it, as it only took him half an hour or so. During the week he went to the library and the park. Sometimes he spent whole days in the precinct, watching the pigeons. He'd heard that the council wanted to move them on. On weekdays he wore his parka, and put the hood up for shelter. He'd noticed that it seemed to keep people away too. On Saturdays he wore his corduroy jacket and combed his hair back with water, into a blackish, brackish, oily DA. He was lucky to get a seat on the bus. Quite a few old people were standing. He got off at the Cenotaph and walked past East Park and Watts Park towards the shops. The Civic Centre clock chimed out the first few bars of 'Oh God Our Help in Ages Past' as he passed the *Titanic* Memorial. Gilbert didn't know that the hymn was by the city's most famous son. He had never heard of Isaac Watts. He thought the chime was something like 'When a Knight Won His Spurs', of which he had vague memories from school. Hefty students were playing football while winos watched them, shouting instructions and jeering them on. What else should you expect if you wear shorts this early in the year?

Gilbert loved the parks, the arrangements, the space to be doing nothing with nobody without anyone noticing. There was a little Chinese bit with bridges and rocks – like a multicoloured willow-pattern plate – where he spent ages wandering, some magnificent conker trees to sit under, and there was talk of restoring a bandstand. There had once been an aviary. The council had taken it down; it was too small, too expensive, too cruel. Azaleas grew where it had stood.

Gilbert went to Asda. He only needed a few staples – bread, milk, Frosties, cheese and onion crisps – things that didn't need cooking. At the precinct he rolled a cigarette. It fitted neatly into a brown stain, but stuck painfully because his lips were chapped. When it was finished he ate a Polo. He sat on a bench and watched the pigeons; children were chasing them with cruel glee. Nobody would talk to Gilbert with his baseball cap pulled right down over his sad, potato face.

He'd chosen a bench opposite Monsoon and Oasis. Pretty young girls went in and out, in and out. He pretended to read his newspaper, and then just sat and stared. Sometimes he sat near New Look; wherever he chose there would be dozens, hundreds to see, marching along in pedal pushers, short skirts, combat trousers, all terrifying.

It began to rain. Gilbert rolled and smoked another cigarette, and wondered what to do next. He tore open the Frosties and pressed a handful into his mouth. Golden dust fell on to his jacket and stuck to the webs of his fingers, and crumbs fell like stars on to his shoes.

4

It was a second Monday and Gilbert's day to sign on. He
wore his anorak because although it was very hot and
sunny, and the sky was utterly cloudless, he expected it to
rain. In his pocket he had an orange-and-black Tango
baseball cap and his orange card, which was very old and
battered and had somehow become stained with egg. He
wrapped it inside his hat to try and stop it from getting
dirtier. A dirty card could lead to loss of benefit for an
unspecified period.

Gilbert had seen lots of changes at the benefit office, but the
spider plants were dying again, and a notice requesting that
customers didn't smoke at the desk still had 'fuck off' scrawled
in a corner. Gilbert queued for fifteen minutes behind a woman
with pale yellow hair that fell around her shoulders like a
shroud. At last he got to the front of the queue, and someone looked at his card and asked him to go to Enquiries.
He went. He queued for another five minutes and then realised
that he was waiting at the wrong window. Eventually he was
seen.

'Mr Gilbert Runnic?' asked a deceptively pretty girl in a not
very clean white blouse. 'Is this your card?'

'Yes. I think so.' He had been holding it just seconds ago. She
picked at the card with a long, sharp nail. Gilbert wondered if
you'd keep hurting yourself with nails like that. He didn't know
that she was playing Titania in the Southampton Amateur

Dramatic Society (SADS) production of *A Midsummer Night's Dream* that night. Her mind was elsewhere.

'Well, it's got egg on it.'

'I'm sorry,' said Gilbert. 'I don't know how that happened.'

'I could hazard a guess,' said the girl. Then: 'Well, Mr Gilbert, it seems that you've been unemployed for a very long time. What steps are you currently taking to procure employment?'

'Oh,' said Gilbert.

'What are you doing to find a job?'

'Oh, looking, mostly,' said Gilbert. This was quite untrue. He had ceased to do more than look in some newsagents' windows some years ago. He was vaguely hoping for a job looking after birds, perhaps at Marwell Zoo which he wanted to visit one day.

'Do you go to the jobcentre?'

'Umm, umm yes! I go every day except Saturdays, I mean Sundays. It's closed then.'

'I know.'

'Got any jobs here then?'

'What qualifications have you got?'

'None.'

'We haven't then.' She started to make a bracelet out of paper clips. Gilbert thought that the interview was over and turned to go.

'Don't just walk away, Mr Gilbert!' she said in a stage whisper. 'Walking away from your problems doesn't work.' She tried out a cheery smile, but failed. Gilbert returned to the counter.

'I'm making an appointment for you to attend a New Deal

Restart interview. The date, time and venue will be notified to you in due course.'

'Thank you,' said Gilbert. 'That's very kind of you.'

In due course Gilbert was informed of the date, time and venue of his Restart interview. It was to be held in an office above the jobcentre. There were three other people there, callow youths. None of them spoke to Gilbert. He watched a video about job clubs, listened to a talk about starting your own business (but to do what?), and drank a cup of vending-machine tea. After that he thought he would be allowed to go, but instead he was taken into a unit of space with plyboard walls and promised a spotty man that he would start attending a job club. In return he would get free coffee, advice, paper, stamps and a seventy per cent chance of finding a job within two years.

'Do they have tea as well?' he asked.

After this Gilbert left. He went back to the Wayside, sat on his bed and looked at his knees. He didn't even have the heart to read *Keeping Finches*. He ate a packet of custard creams and then got into bed.

The next day it drizzled and Gilbert left his room only to visit the lavatory at the end of the corridor. He read his books and listened to the baby crying behind the wall. He washed a shirt and some socks and pants, and hung them on the radiator where they didn't dry, but gave off a warm and comforting vapour.

He could have spent the evening in the TV lounge, watching programmes chosen by tougher, more popular residents. By the end of each evening empty cans lay around the room like very small sleeping dogs. Gilbert would put his own cans in the dustbin liner in the corner and shuffle off to bed. A few people would mutter, 'G'night, Gilbert', and he'd half raise a hand in resignation as much as farewell.

The following day it poured and Gilbert decided to go out and even to look for a job. He always went out when it rained because there was rarely anyone about, just deranged women carrying drenched baskets. He walked around town, then, motivated by the free tea, he crossed the city to Shirley, walked up Shirley High Street to where the job club was held. One of the only people ever to do what he was told at a Restart interview.

5

After eight and a half years of unemployment, Gilbert's job-hunting was suddenly successful. The job club was held in a disused church. The pews had been ripped out and sold, and Gilbert sat in a white plastic garden chair and looked at newspapers and drank cups of tea. After a few weeks he applied for two jobs, both with the City Council who claimed to pursue a policy of Equal Opportunities. It seemed that they did, because although Gilbert was short, dandruffy and had no formal qualifications, he was offered a job as a Refuse Sack Delivery Person. Perhaps the years he'd spent in a Sheltered Workshop painting miniature cottages had equipped him with the 'transferable skills' the interviewers were looking for, perhaps it was the endless days he'd spent shuffling around Southampton; Gilbert didn't know what did it, but he was very pleased.

He rose at six each weekday morning and missed the Wayside's cooked breakfast. He walked to the depot where the dustcarts lurked beside huge sheds and a site manager gave him an allocation of bags. He rode in splendour to each of the day's areas. His job was to walk through the streets and drag the full bin bags into gangs on street corners and leave the shiny new liners for people to find in 'easily accessible places'. He shoved them through holes in gates and wedged them in fences and letter boxes. He had to work fast to keep ahead of the dustcart and the rest of the crew. He risked their wrath if they caught up with him. They aimed to be home and cleaned up as early as possible. His job was tiring and dirty. Despite gloves and his cap, his hands, hair, his whole self smelled permanently of garbage. The bin bags split or sometimes were left open so that nappies, cat litter, tea bags and cans with jagged edges cascaded on to his council-issue boots. The men who followed him, heaving the sacks into the truck, were brawny and matey. Sometimes they joked with him and called him Bert the Bags, but his inferior role as a bagger and dragger meant that he was never really one of the lads. His lack of height and strength made promotion unlikely.

After a while Gilbert got into the swing of the bins. It was sunny and he began to love his job. He became familiar with his rounds and knew each garden, which hedges had birds in, the friendliest cats and who put out the neatest sacks. He tried to be speedy. There was hope of leaving the Wayside (but where for?) and the daily pleasure of lunch at the council canteen, which was very cheap.

Gilbert could choose from dozens of dishes. Not everything was swamped by grease or water, there were great puddings, and exotic things like moussaka, chicken tikka in sandwiches, and pasta that wasn't macaroni cheese. Sometimes they had theme days and the canteen ladies pretended to be Spanish or French or even Mexican. He filled his pockets with sachets of sugar and little tubs of UHT cream.

Gilbert heard that people gave the binmen tips at Christmas and he hoped his job would last that long. At the Wayside he became one of the workers, and some people envied him. He wished that he, like the cake packers, could bring home spoils, but the only things he found and kept were books with mould-spotted covers. He picked over the remains of shoes, but they were always the wrong size (few men take a six and a half) or were too blatantly women's. One day he found a Chinese paper parasol that smelled deliciously of toxic paint. It was decorated with peacocks, and although it was stiff to open and had a spoke missing, he took it back to the Wayside, intending to give it to the girl next door – she could use it to shield her baby from the sun – he just had to catch her eye first.

On Saturdays Gilbert didn't lurk in the precinct any more. He slept late and just went to the park instead. His crew had yet to ask him out for a drink, but they seemed pleased enough to see him each morning and no longer yelled at him for being slow. At night he had no trouble getting to sleep.

Gilbert was fascinated by the homes where he left his sacks. He loved going into other people's gardens; he'd rarely got beyond the gates before. On Wednesdays his round was on home turf, the inner city, the poorest part, the former red-light district, which was now populated by students, Asian families, and a few drug dealers and prostitutes. The houses were crumbling Victorian and Edwardian, homes built for dockers. In one window a Barbie in a cut-off wedding dress stared sadly into the road. Gilbert didn't know that she was inviting people into a brothel. There were mango stones – huge, hairy – sucked lozenges in the gutters, and students' bikes with detached wheels chained up in the yards. Gilbert was thankful that the Wayside had huge industrial-size bins – he didn't have to drag that rubbish on to the pavement. He'd lived in the area for years, but he was only now up early enough to see its secret early-morning world. At a quarter to nine (early by local time) a trickle of children started on their way to school. It soon became a flutter, a flurry. The girls wore silky suits in vivid and pastel colours. Gilbert would stop to watch them, a flock of butterflies, of magic hummingbirds, nourished on coriander, pistachios, jalabis and 10p mix-up, while lollipop ladies directed them safely across the paths of juggernauts. The girls ran through the dust in their patent-leather shoes, their glossy black plaits beat against their sugared-almond backs. Who were these beautiful creatures of the morning, Gilbert wondered, and why were they always wearing party dresses?

As Gilbert grew used to his job he became more and more familiar with individual houses. He could tell who had cats or children, who was neat. Each house was meant to get two bags, businesses got more, but Gilbert started to award extra bags to houses with nice gardens or children or cats. He penalised houses whose bags were split or filled with empty Skona lager cans and bottles. Points were lost if an expensive car or, even worse, a windsurfer was outside, or if the front garden looked newly concreted over. Children's bicycles were worth an extra sack, hedges with birds' nests scored the highest. After a while some houses were getting four or five bags a week, others none. Gilbert was annoyed by tardiness, so the Bluebird Café lost out.

Gilbert liked the exterior of the Bluebird, the pretty painted sign and the bright colours. He wanted to go in, but it never, ever seemed to be open. It claimed to open at eleven o'clock, but Gilbert was beginning to have his doubts. It was closed on Sundays, and closed at 9 p.m. each night.

'What about breakfast?' he railed against its bolted door whenever he passed. What sort of café didn't bother to open? If Gilbert had a café like that he'd open at seven sharp every morning, come rain or shine. There would be tea and toast and Full English Breakfast all day. He got angrier with it as the weeks passed, leaving them four, then three, then two and then no bags at all.

6

'Lucy, can I ask you, what's this about?' John Vir handed her a crumpled bit of computer printout. SOUTHAMP-TON CENTRAL COLLEGE STUDENT'S INTERIM REPORT. The creases had turned grey.

'Are you sure you want me to see this? Gurpal might mind.'

'I'd like to know what you think,' he told her. Gurpal was at the back of the shop, within yelling distance as usual.

'It might be personal,' Lucy said.

'But what do you think?'

Lucy read on, but silently. Then looked up, embarrassed. She was aware of John Vir peering intently at her.

'Well, she is doing well with Keyboard Skills and Childcare, isn't she? Cs are good.'

'And the rest?'

'D for Domestic Science. That's not too bad, is it? But maybe you should ask her about the Media Studies, Computing and Business Administration. Perhaps they aren't her best subjects. There might be something she'd enjoy doing more.'

'What was it she got again?'

Lucy wondered if he found it hard to read the report, or perhaps the tatty computer printout was confusing, or perhaps he just wanted her opinion.

'Oh, um, well, Fs,' she said.

'Her mother has written wanting news. What do I tell her?

27

And what's this?' He handed her another crumpled slip, like an old-style credit-card voucher.

'Well, I wouldn't give the college a very high grade for presentation,' Lucy said, but he didn't seem to think that was funny.

Dear Mr and Mrs Vir,

Appointment with GURPAL VIR'S personal tutor. Please attend on 26/6 at 18.40 p.m. to discuss your child's progress with his/her personal tutor. Meetings will last approximately $8\frac{1}{2}$ minutes and will take place in the students homebase room. The student is encouraged to attend with you.

Yours sincerely,

Trisha Copperplate (Mrs)

College Liaison Secretary

'Well, that's tonight, isn't it? I think you and Gurpal should go. Then you could write and tell Mrs Vir what they say. Perhaps Gurpal's missing her. You could tell her that.'

'Hmm.' John Vir looked as though it hadn't occurred to him that his daughter might miss her mother whom she hadn't seen for almost five years.

'Perhaps I should send her to join her.'

'Mightn't Mrs Vir come back?' Lucy asked.

'I don't think so.'

'Perhaps if she knew how Gurpal was feeling.'

'She bought a one-way ticket.'

'Oh.'

Lucy remembered to pay for her shopping (eggs, five tins of

chickpeas, three bunches of coriander, a veggie samosa as a surprise for Paul) and left.

'Gurpal, come here!'

Gurpal shuffled towards him, her mouth full of Monster Munch.

'Gurpal, we're going to your college tonight to talk to personal tutor at 18.40 p.m.'

'Aw, Dad, why? We never went before.'

'You never told me about it before. This came in the post.' He fluttered the printouts at her.

'None of the other dads will go.'

'Your mother has written for news on you.'

'What does she care? She never sends us anything.'

'Why do they have sawdust in buckets? That's not going to put out a fire,' John Vir asked. He was one of the only dads there.

'For when people are sick in the corridor,' Gurpal explained.

'Does that happen often?'

'Yeah.'

It wasn't that surprising. The place stank of Impulse, school disinfectant, photocopying, mud and sick. There were displays of trophies and photos of what looked like the dreariest field trips ever to some flat beaches. In Gurpal's Homebase room, which was also the Domestic Science room, were some more interesting displays on Home Technology.

'Which bits are yours?' he asked.

'Um, my class did this.'

Gurpal's diagrams of 'How To Change A Plug' had ended up in the bin. She had confused the earth and live wires and been ridiculed by the teacher, a small Welsh rodent whose neat

29

pink fingers itched to cut off Gurpal's oiled plait and trim the results into a neat and practical bob. She had seen Gurpal's filthy pink hairbrush and longed to give it a good soak in Dettox. Gurpal wasn't one of her favourites.

'Well, I certainly shan't be asking to borrow your hairdryer, Gurpal!' her singsong voice had chimed across the desks.

Gurpal replied in Punjabi: 'Wouldn't let you, bitch.'

The next project was entitled 'More Safety in the Home'.

'I did some of this, Dad,' Gurpal told him. 'I'll show you my file.' Gurpal's file wasn't one of the ones prominently displayed on Mrs Jones's desk. Gurpal found it in a pile under a double-glazed window where a wasp and two bluebottles had met their ends.

'Here it is, Dad.' Flecks of Crunchie stuck between the pages marked the file as her own.

'I didn't know you did this stuff.' John Vir was impressed.

There was a project on baby equipment and one on poisons. 'Don't be testing either of these out.'

' "Some Common Household Poissons." ' (He read to himself.)

Bleech
Some Detergens
Cleaning Fluid
Are all very poissonous and should be kept in a safe place.
A locked cupboard is a good idea.
Plants and Berrys such as hollyberry and missletoe, laburnam pods ect. also corse death and upset tummies. Salmonelle is a major corse of poissoning. Cook meat and eggs properly. Store food cold. Cooked food on top of raw

food in the fridge too avoid contaminating with bood and germs.

Cook Food Properly.

Cook all eggs hard and don't use raw ones or lick fingers or eat cake mix. Cook meat for the right anmount and don't heat it up again too many times. Make the oven is hot enough too.

Undercooking food kills too. Kidney beans must cook for 4 hour or more.'

'Is that right?'

'What?' said Gurpal.

'Kidney beans can kill you.'

'What?'

'That's what you put here.'

'We copied it off leaflets.'

'Must be true then.'

'Yeah.'

'Food for thought,' said John Vir, and he realised that he'd made his daughter smile.

'Come on,' he said, 'I'll get you some chips on the way home.'

They left arm in arm, forgetting their $8\frac{1}{2}$ minutes with Mrs Jones.

As John Vir lay sleepless and itchy under the orange quilted polyester bedspread that had been part of his wife's dowry, he thought about getting rid of Paul, about raw eggs and under-cooked meat. But how could you make anyone eat a raw egg? Hold them down and force them to swallow it? You couldn't put it in their tea. Undercooked meat wouldn't do. He knew

31

that Lucy and Paul didn't eat meat, and tricking a vegetarian would be wrong. But then poisoning was wrong really, he told himself. He kicked off the covers and stretched out his long, strong legs. Kidney beans might work though . . . a dinner party . . . or could he make something and take it round? But what if Lucy ate it and died too? He could sell Paul a poisoned Mars bar, some sort of chocolate that Lucy didn't like. Or give him a cup of tea with ground glass. How did you grind glass? Was there a machine you could hire? How much per day? It was no good, he'd be caught.

7

M avis liked to sit on the low breeze-block wall beside her flat. It caught the sun for most of the day. Sometimes she read her magazine, but mostly she accosted passers-by. A real local character, she had a cheery word for everybody. Sensitive souls made long detours to avoid her.

'Been shopping?' she yelled at people struggling by with bursting carriers and breaking arms. 'You'll never get rich that way!' she joked each time.

If it was raining she'd mostly stay indoors, only rushing out to yell 'Lovely weather . . . for ducks!' at anyone she knew. Or if it was icy, she skidded out to warn the postman not to slip on her short path, even though she didn't get much post, just catalogues mostly.

Gilbert delivered her sacks, but as her flat was near the depot she wasn't often up in time to see the binmen. She made sure that she remembered everybody at Christmas. She balanced some mince pies on top of her dustbin. They were lovely ones, Kipling's, really fruity. She knew that the binmen would like those. Getting up early must make you really hungry. Gilbert was the only one to eat those mince pies. The others wanted to sling them in the cart.

'How do you know they're not rubbish? There might be something in them!' said Jim, a kind-hearted driver who always tried to look out for Gilbert. He could see that Gilbert wasn't all there. But Gilbert knew Kipling's. He'd been eating them all year for years. Christmas past and present met up somewhere in July. Sell-by dates were generous, and his fellow residents at the Wayside brought the pies home by the pallet. Christmas yet to come would bring Mavis's home-made mincies. Mavis loved mince pies, bought or made, anything with mincemeat, or anything with pastry. She could make her own pastry too. She fluted her pies by pressing the charcoal moons of her nails all around the edges.

8

M avis had a problem with her front door. It had a glass panel at the bottom, as flimsy as paper. People broke these panels. They kicked them in on the way back from the pubs. If the panel was kicked in then someone could get into the flat, and what if that happened? They'd be after her collections, she knew it.

Councillor Bette Doon was sitting behind a yellow Formica table in the Community Drop-in, reading *Woman's Weekly* and deciding to call it a day if nobody showed up in the next five minutes. Her Residents' Surgery Mornings on the Golden Grove estate were ailing. Cllr Doon had represented her ward for eighteen years and had been Mayoress twice. She had huge, melting, pink features, springy grey hair, and the most supportive hose that money could buy.

Mavis stomped in wearing a huge black T-shirt with seal cubs, a beige canvas skirt that no longer buttoned through and a pair of Totes slipper socks. It wasn't really raining that heavily . . .

'It's about our doors,' she announced as she plonked herself down in the chair opposite Cllr Doon. 'These panels. They're as flimsy as paper! It's only a matter of time before someone is murdered in her bed. There have been three break-ins in three weeks and they kick the panels in when they're pissed up.'

'Have you talked to the housing office about this?'

'I'm telling you. Want to come and see? It's only round the corner.'

'Very well, my dear.' Bette Doon always tried to oblige. They walked around the corner to Mavis's flat.

Mavis was right about the panels; they were a disgrace. Cllr Doon said she'd raise the matter with the Chair of Housing. Mavis seemed satisfied for now.

'Stay for a cuppa,' she said.

The mugs were red with BOVRIL in white block letters. Bette found it disconcerting, expecting beefy goodness and tasting tea. She pretended she'd finished and carried her mug into the kitchen and tipped the Bovril-tea down the sink.

'When did this happen? It's terrible! Did they take much?'

A large hole had been smashed through one of the panes of the window beside the sink. Some orange knitting was wadded over the jagged edges and held in place by parcel tape.

'That's my DIY cat flap,' Mavis grinned. 'Took one minute and saved a tenner. Now Boots can come and go as she pleases. Before I was always getting up to let her in and out. Not any more!'

9

'**I** 've buried two. Well, burned them. Cremated, you know,' Mavis explained as she tucked into her beef casserole with dumplings, rice, chips and sweetcorn. She had lurked in the Civic Centre foyer, and lurked, until she had seen Bette.

'Nice to see you!' Bette said heartily as she came down the stairs from the Council Chamber. They were worthy of a Busby Berkeley sequence, and Bette was always slightly nervous of slipping. The strange-looking woman (or could it possibly be someone in drag?) looked familiar. Mavis had leaped up beaming.

'Waiting to see someone?'

'You of course. About them panels.'

(Ah, the Bovril cat-flap woman.)

'I'll be on to the housing office again this afternoon. They should have been in touch with you by now.' The panels had completely slipped her mind. Now, what was the name of that obliging girl in Housing? The one with the green headband. She always seemed to jump. Bette had started walking briskly towards the canteen, then realised that Mavis was loping along beside her.

'What the hell,' she had thought. 'What harm could standing this poor soul some lunch possibly do?'

Mavis was wearing a pale blue T-shirt with a woodland scene and the legend 'I Love Wildlife' stretched across her stomach.

Gilbert was drawn towards the picture, the cute squirrels, and sat down at the same table, his eyes fixed on the many soft bulges of Mavis's chest. Gilbert thought that anyone who wore that T-shirt must be kind and good. He smiled as he spooned the day's special, Italian meatballs, into his mouth.

'What are you looking at then?' Mavis suddenly demanded, thinking that she was being eyed up.

'Who, me?' Gilbert was shocked at being spoken at, frightened too. He came every day after his shift, but nobody ever talked to him.

'You staring at me?'

'I was just looking at your nice squirrels.'

'This sounds too much like a *Carry On*. I've got to be in Committee in five minutes. I'll let you know about the panels. Goodbye.' Bette made a speedy exit.

Gilbert saw that Mavis was smiling, not cross.

'I got this one at Aldi in the Valley. £3.99. Glad you like it.' She thrust her chest towards him provocatively.

'It's nice,' said Gilbert. 'I like all animals.'

He showed Mavis where to put her tray and then where the exit was. He'd finished for the day and was heading back to the Wayside for a snooze.

'Which way you going then?' Mavis asked him.

'Across the park.'

'My way too,' she said.

'You want to get on the housing list,' Mavis said when he told her that he lived at the Wayside.

'Would they have anywhere for me? Isn't it for families?'

'No. For anyone. Aren't you in a family then?' she asked.

'No.'

10

M avis was starting a new collection. She got the *South-ampton News* every day and looked through it for pictures or just articles with any reference to Cllr Doon. She picked up extra copies of the council's own tabloid publicity paper and snipped out the pictures, councillors' surgery times and committee dates and pasted them into a special scrapbook. She stuck the double-page spread of the councillors' pictures and their phone numbers (some even gave home phone numbers) on the wall beside the phone.

'That'll be handy,' she said.

One day there was even a photo of Bette on the front page of the *News*, opening the new paddling pool. She wasn't wearing a swimsuit, but she was in bare feet, up to her knees in the pretty ripples. A community worker, just out of shot, was holding her sandals. Children who'd won prizes in a colouring competition jostled her to be among the first into the pool and at the front of the photo. Mavis ordered a blown-up copy of that photo from the *News* office. £2.50. She framed it in a knobbly frame that she'd crocheted herself from purple sparkly yarn.

Cllr Doon sank down into one of the soft blue leather armchairs in the Labour Member's Room and took out her list of Things to Do.

– Talk to J about rat-runs.
– Committee apologies.

- Foundations.
- Signpost outside Mrs De Silva's. Movable?
- Door panels. Replacements?
- Reschedule governors.
- Ring Gangwarily Youth Leaders.
- Tallest sunflower. Delegate?
- Health Commission Qs & As.
- Talk to Minnie re photocopier.
- Draft Library Users' Charter. Ditch?

Where to start, where to start? She wondered if it would be possible for a Councillor to do nothing at all, to just reschedule and give apologies and set up meetings and delegate and achieve nothing without anybody ever noticing. She thought that it probably would. She reached for a phone. Now, what was the name of that keen little housing girl with the green headband?

'Housing Strategy. How can I help you?'

'Rachel?' she barked.

'No, it's Rebecca. There isn't a Rachel in Housing Strategy, but people are always calling *me* Rachel.'

'Sorry, my dear, I meant Rebecca.'

'That's OK. I usually just answer to Rachel as well.'

'It's Bette Doon here.'

'How can I help you, Councillor?'

'I've had some queries about doors and windows in Golden Grove. Apparently, they're a soft target for vandals. Lots of break-ins too. Don't have any statistics, but people just don't feel safe.'

'Oh dear,' said Rachel-Rebecca, pushing her headband, which that day was black velvet early Hillary Clinton-style, back into position. The phone always nudged it sideways.

'Oh dear is right, my dear. Now, isn't there some scheme or other about replacing them?' Cllr Doon asked.

'Yes, we're replacing them all over the next year. All windows and doors in Golden Grove and Albion Towers will be UPVC by the millennium. That's our target. Should solve some condensation problems too, and maybe reduce the incidence of asthma, according to the Tenants' Association.'

'When exactly does it start then?'

'Albion Towers in two months. Then Golden Grove in numerical order. Odds first.'

'So when would 167 West Walk be done?' Cllr Doon asked.

'I can look it up. Do you want me to call you back?'

'No, look it up now please, Rachel, I'm in a hurry with this one.'

'OK, won't be long.' Then silence, then a sound of something heavy being dumped down, rustling, rustling. What was the girl doing? Eating crisps? Then: 'Here it is. West Walk is after Josian Walk, after Albion Towers.'

'OK. So when would number 167 be done?'

'About four months from now?'

'Good girl. Well done. When will you be telling the tenants?'

'They should already know from posters on the wardens' boards and an article in *Tenants Together*, but they'll get their own letters too, four weeks before the scheduled start.'

'Jolly good. Send me a copy of the works schedule when it's out, won't you? Goodbye.'

'Mavis? Councillor Doon here.'

Mavis made a little noise like a balloon being let off. Bette was unable to tell from where it had emitted.

'I've sorted out your door and windows, my dear. They'll be done within the next four months. You'll get a letter about the exact date, and nice new white UPVC replacements. They'll solve any condensation troubles too, for you and all of your neighbours. I hope you're pleased with that. Now, no more home-made cat flaps! Let me know if I can help with anything else.'

Mavis was stunned.

'Thank you, Councillor,' she said. She hadn't expected Cllr Doon to ring her up herself like a real friend, much too busy with the councilling. And arranging all that for her.

'Shows it's not what you know, it's who you know,' Mavis told Boots, as she tucked into her meaty chunks.

A week later Bette was sitting on one of the pretty 1930s benches outside the Council Chamber, checking through some papers before what might be a crucial committee meeting.

'I've took you as good as your word.' A shadow fell over her papers, her light was blocked.

'Hmm?' Cllr Doon raised her eyes from the copy of 'Southampton On Thin Ice', a residents' group manifesto. They wanted an ice rink but wouldn't accept that in this day and age it was up to the private sector to take the lead. Perhaps the new bowling alley would shut them up. She didn't really expect so. Cllr Doon sometimes wished that young people could be allowed to hang around on street corners. They always used to, but now people thought that there was something wrong with it, that they should be quietly or noisily occupied somewhere else, or at least in somebody else's neighbourhood. And even the ones who were allowed to hang around on the streets were allocated Detached Youth Workers, whatever they were. Brightly coloured structures called Hang-abouts had even been installed on some of the city's estates so that the young people could have some official focus for their hanging about. Perhaps she was getting old . . . and now here was that window-woman come to bother her. Some people were never satisfied.

'Yes?' She managed a smile, but pointedly, she hoped, didn't put down her papers or offer a seat. There wouldn't have been room for their two amply spreading behinds on the elegant little bench anyway.

'You said that if I needed help with anything . . .' Mavis began.

'Did I?' Bette asked (surely not!). 'And how can I help?'

'Look at this. It's laughing at you. Ha ha! I just came in to pay the poll tax and I caught my foot on the steps there, and now it's split, innit. Got any glue here?'

Mavis plonked her foot up on the bench next to the bag which contained Bette's Marks and Spencer's food shopping. At least it was all pre-packaged. The ancient pink-and-grey trainer had split, the sole flapped hideously, revealing the knob of a big toe in a whitish towelling sock of the sort that Bette imagined some men might wear to play sports.

'I'm afraid that I don't carry glue,' said Cllr Doon, but her scathing tone was lost on Mavis who was twitching her toe up and down, up and down, making the hole even bigger.

'Where's the council glue cupboard then? I am a ratepayer, you know.'

'The council doesn't usually take responsibility for people's footwear.'

'Did it on council property, didn't I.' Mavis looked as though she might get violent.

Would a pound coin send her on her way? I'll just shout for security, Bette told herself, although she knew that it would take at least ten minutes for the council's security guards to stub out their cigarettes in their coffee-jar-lid ashtrays and come lumbering up the stairs to apprehend the wrong person. She sighed.

11

P aul had spent a whole weekend bent double painting hopping frogs on the wide tarmac path that led to the Badger Centre. As he completed the last one some boys zoomed past his paint pot, their rollerblades missing it by a millimetre. He stared after them and saw that his bright green frogs looked as though they had been squashed by a stream of traffic. Oh well. The end of the line for the frogs. He lifted the stencil to reveal that he had smudged the last frog's fingers. He considered finding a pot of pink and adding a lipsticky smile and some varnished fingernails to cover it up. He picked up the paint stuff and followed the frog trail towards the Centre. Paul loved the automatic doors. He thought of them as magic, and he smiled as he breathed in the Centre's special smell of school trips, mice, crayons and sugar paper, seeds and aquaria. If ants had a smell, it would be there too.

The Centre Manager, Madelaine, was sitting at the desk with Kirsty, a work-experience girl, who they hoped might stay on as a volunteer. She was developing a crush on Paul, so she probably would.

'Hi, Paul!' said Kirsty. He wondered why as they had already said hello to each other that morning. He and Madelaine just nodded at each other when the need arose.

'Finished the frogs,' he told them. 'They look squashed though.'

'Never mind,' said Madelaine. 'Nobody's going to really look at them, are they?'

'I guess not,' said Paul.

'Kirsty's been clearing out the mice,' Madelaine told him.

'Could she have a go at the noticeboard? Lots of things are out of date,' he said.

'I did it this morning,' Kirsty pouted.

'Well, the hawk display was a month ago. And this sponsored walk's long gone. And the Owl Talk. Could you put the Birdsong Seminar in the middle, with the Bank Holiday Bug Hunt?' Madelaine added.

'Awright, Mad Elaine,' Kirsty sighed, drawing out the syllables. She had wanted to do her work experience at Marwell Zoo, but they'd been full up. At least she wasn't stuck in a rest home like her friend Nicky. That's what they gave you if you didn't put your form in on time, even if you were allergic to the sight of blood. This Paul Cloud was pretty gorgeous, with his long legs and crooked smile, and his sandy hair always messed up, like he'd just got out of bed; but it couldn't stop her from getting bored. She'd already cleaned out all the tanks and hung up some stuff for the birds and fed the fish. This Mad Elaine was bossy too. And now she was going into a huddle with Paul. Kirsty tried to look unconcerned, and started to line up the magnetic badgers (45p each); but she could still hear old Mad Elaine telling Paul that she had handed in her notice and she was moving to Norfolk and a job at some duck place. Then she heard Paul say: 'I'm sure working with wildfowl will really suit you.' He didn't even mean it as an insult! And then he gave Mad Elaine his really nice smile, and she hugged him.

'Who's the boss if you're not here?' Kirsty asked later.

'Well, the Chair of the Committee, I suppose,' Madelaine told her.

'Is that Paul Cloud?' Kirsty asked. She wanted to test out saying his name.

'No. Paul's just on the Committee. He's a volunteer. At the moment.'

12

The young Lucy Brookes thought that she came from a Bohemian Background. Her mother Jane played the piano and gave lessons and had tablemats with scenes of Montmartre.

When she was ten Lucy joined a group called 'Young Stagers'. They put on productions of *Annie* and *Oliver!*, and gave afternoon shows to Old Folk and the Handicapped. Lucy longed for a career on the stage, but her talents went largely undiscovered, and she remained trapped as Third Urchin and Fifth Orphan, while other blonder, smaller children hogged the limelight. She had occasional turns in variety shows, but was more often left in the wings, and spent most of each performance peering through tears in the curtains at the audience nodding and dozing. After the curtain went down the Young Stagers were instructed to chat to the audience. Lucy would pass around sausage rolls and have nothing to say, so she'd ask old men what they'd done in the war. After tea the old people would sing songs.

It was late November. The time for old folks' Christmas parties. Were they held so early to get them over with, or to ensure that as many of the potential guests as possible made it to the party before they died? Didn't it matter that the party was nowhere near actual Christmas? If your life was so empty that you were on the guest list, then would you be past caring anyway? Lucy was nearly twelve and beginning to wonder about such things. A man was asleep beside his accordion. A woman without much hair nudged Lucy.

'Wake him up! He'll want to sing "Paddy McGinty's Goat"! He'll want to sing "Paddy McGinty's Goat"!' she shouted. A chorus of others joined in. Lucy went over to the man.

'Sir,' she said. 'Sir.' She tapped his hand. It wasn't very warm.

'His name's Eric. Wake him up!' yelled the woman.

'Wake up, Eric!' said Lucy. 'They want you to sing.' She shook his shoulder.

Eric fell forward and out of his chair. Yellow stuff came out of his mouth and nose and went on Lucy's skirt.

'Oh, he's gone! He's gone!' said the woman. The chorus joined in. Lucy tried to sit him up, but he was too heavy. Eric's accordion fell off its chair and landed with a discord of despair. Lucy felt the yellow stuff on her legs. Mobile adults came to her aid. An ambulance was called.

'At least he made it to the party,' one of the ambulancemen remarked.

After that Lucy quit the boards. She also quit Sunday school. The doll's house went undecorated that Christmas. Its inhabitants lay slumped in drunken attitudes against the walls, with only a paste bowl of fruit for sustenance.

Lucy announced on Christmas morning that she had become a vegetarian, and that caused trouble. She became insular and sulky, and hung around the house like one of the abandoned doll's house people. In the spring she decided to become a gardener. She grew pots of geraniums, sunflowers, marigolds and tiny cacti from seeds. The runner beans had a bumper crop and Lucy cooked them and served them with lashings of melted margarine. Her father speared them on his meaty fork and pronounced them 'very good indeed'. Then she cooked other things – cheese straws, jam tarts, Victoria sponges, banana cakes – tins and tins of stuff that nobody would eat. She started to take cookery books out of the library and experimented with grown-up food. When she was fifteen she got an A in her Home Economics O level, and considered going to catering college, but the thought of all that meat put her off, and anyway, she already knew how to cook. Instead she took A levels in English, History of Art, History and Home Economics. She went to university in Southampton to study English. She met Paul. Life was going to be one long tea party.

13

Paul's family lived in Sussex. They had moved there from Penshurst, a little village just outside Southampton, when Paul was fourteen. They all thought it interesting that Paul had seemingly moved back to his roots when he chose his university. Paul said that the Southampton University course looked the most interesting. His father, James Cloud, taught Latin and had curly grey hair and a penchant for sandals, not open-toed Jesus Creepers, but woven ones, French ones. He bought a pair every year at La Rochelle. His mother, Maggie, had very neat hair and favoured wraparound skirts. They liked the theatre, and living near Chichester meant that they saw a few good shows each year without having to brave the crowds and noise of the West End and the homeless at Victoria. That's what they told their friends.

Start-Rite shoes had been Paul's lot. A liking for sensible shoes seemed to be genetic, and even when he was at his most rebellious – going off to school with a pair of drainpipes hidden under the flappy John Lewis uniform trousers Maggie had so carefully picked out for him, and so carefully sewn the name tapes into – he still wore a pair of desert boots which he'd Scotchgarded himself. He had a green canvas rucksack adopted from a friend. 'David Bowie' had been black marker-penned on the flap and was now fading to grey. Paul went through a phase of trying to skive and muck around, but he couldn't help accidentally learning things and ending up with straight As. He was embarrassingly good at Geography and Biology. He tried and tried, but he could always remember how artesian wells were made, the difference between taiga and tundra, the names and positions of the Great Lakes, the main stops on the Trans-Siberian railway. The cross-section through a dogfish was a doddle, phloem and xylem flowed through his fingers. He could draw a perfect diagram of the heart and got a starred Grade 1 for his S-level Biology.

The Clouds really hit it off with Lucy's family, the Brookeses. Lucy's mum talked to Paul's mum about music. They all discussed programmes on Radio 4, gardening and The Theatre. They made jokes in Latin, which Lucy suspected her dad had been cramming from a *Past Times* catalogue desk diary. Lucy and Paul made deliberate efforts to keep the two families apart. They thought the Clouds and Brookeses would start ganging up on them, dropping collective hints about weddings and grand-children, and the importance of Buying a House.

14

Lucy was becoming more and more irritable. The café
broke even, just, but only if she paid Abigail a pittance and
she and Paul lived on the customers' leftovers. She was always
tired and could never stop her hands from smelling of tinned
tomatoes, even though she had bought herself a very expensive
soap-sized and -shaped chunk of steel from the Divertimenti
catalogue. The lump was reputedly used by all the top chefs
who didn't want their hands smelling of onion.

It was 8.30 a.m., Paul was still asleep. The pilot light had gone
out in the boiler and there was no hot water for a bath. She opened
the curtains and saw a small, grubby, funny-looking man pulling
their rubbish into the gutter. She thought he was stealing it. Then
she realised that he was one of the binmen, a council bag-
deliverer. He stood and stared at the Bluebird with what looked
like contempt and then he hitched his satchel of binbags higher on
his shoulder and walked on. He hadn't left them any bags.

She opened the window and leaned out.

'Hey! Where are our bags?'

Gilbert turned to see a beautiful girl in not many clothes
hanging out of a window and TALKING TO HIM.

'Give us some bags or I'll write to the council!' yelled Lucy.
Gilbert fled.

'What are you doing now, fishwife?' Paul had woken to ask.
She turned to see his loose pink morning mouth, the reddish
stubble around the gills, the bleary eyes.

'Fishwife is right,' she said, and stomped off.

She crushed pilchards for Fennel, sniffed her hands again. More tinned tomato and fishwife hands. Paul appeared in the kitchen and they were lost in the routine of the day. She felt faintly guilty for being rude to the bag-deliverer, but then he hadn't been doing his job, was probably selling their bags or something. She cleaned the café while Paul cleaned some vegetables. At 11.30 they put on the coffee and unlocked the door. Someone was waiting. The funny-looking man.

'Hello,' said Lucy.

'Are you open yet?'

'Yes. Just opening now.'

'I brought you some bags.'

'Thank you. We do use lots, but we never get our share.'

'Why don't you open for breakfast? A lot of people need their breakfast, you know.' Gilbert continued to stand blocking the doorway. He handed Lucy a wad of bin bags.

'But there are dozens here.'

'It's your share. Don't tell the council, please.' He looked desperate.

'Tell the council what?' said Paul, appearing behind Lucy, eating a wedge of toast and peanut butter, and feeling voluble.

'I've got a lot to tell the council,' he said, mouth full, peanut-butter breath. Gilbert blanched beyond the colour of dough. 'They spray the hedges with pesticide,' Paul went on between bites. 'It's so strong that a man has to wear a spacesuit. I suppose it's a man anyway.'

'What else would it be?' asked Lucy. 'Robo-employee?'

'I saw a goldfinch eating stuff they'd just sprayed. I've been meaning to write to them for weeks.'

'A goldfinch? Where?' Gilbert forgot to be nervous.

'In that car park, by the Six Dials roundabout,' Paul told him. Gilbert looked ready to rush off and see, but Paul said, 'Are you interested in birds? Come in. Be our first customer of the day. There's some coffee on already.'

'Tea, please,' said Gilbert. Lucy moved aside and Gilbert stepped over the threshold of the Bluebird Café.

'What sort of tea?' said Lucy.

'Lots of milk and three,' said Gilbert. He hadn't noticed the enamel canisters labelled from 'Almond' to 'Zinger – Orange'. The urn spluttered and Lucy handed him a bowl of brown rocks. Gilbert was confused.

'Sugar,' she said. 'That's 50p.'

'On the house,' said Paul.

'Do you like birds and animals then?' said Gilbert.

'Yes. I'm doing my PhD on climatic change and hedgehogs' prickles,' said Paul. Gilbert looked blank again, but Paul didn't notice.

'But why don't you do breakfast?' Gilbert asked.

'We do brunch,' said Lucy. 'And Vegetarian All Day Breakfast.'

'But too late,' said Gilbert. 'I could come if you opened early.'

'Perhaps you should open up earlier, Lucy,' said Paul.

'I don't think so,' said Lucy, standing behind the counter, Happy Shopper J-cloth in hand, looking fierce. 'There wouldn't be much demand.'

'Well, I'd come. And some of the men on the bins. And from the hotel.'

'Hotel?'

'The Wayside. Where I live.' For Lucy the name conjured up

men sitting on steps with cider bottles, mattresses rotting, and regular fires reported in the local papers: DERELICTS' DEATH-TRAP and LANDLORD BROKE RULES.

'Well, since my baby left me . . .' hummed Paul.

'Paul!' hissed Lucy. 'We work so hard in the evenings,' she told Gilbert. 'I couldn't get up early too.'

'Not that early,' said Gilbert. 'I could help . . .'

'But you've got a job,' said Lucy very quickly.

'Aren't you writing to the council then?'

'Oh, she never writes to the council. Don't worry,' said Paul.

'I have brought you some bags now,' said Gilbert. 'And I'll always give you yours now.'

'OK,' said Lucy. 'Thank you.'

'That goldfinch . . .' said Gilbert.

Ten minutes later they were all sitting round a table writing letters to the council.

Dear Sir or Madam,

I am writing to you about the city council's use of deadly chemicals in areas of natural environmental importance. Recently I witnessed a person, whom I assumed to be a council worker, dressed in a spacesuit and spraying the area around the Six Dials' car park. This, as you should be aware, is an area that, despite being scrubby and somewhat littered, supports a number of interesting and beautiful plant species including poppies, thistles, grasses, ragwort and willowherb, and a number of garden escapees. I saw the council worker deliberately spraying the thistledown on which the goldfinches feed. I shudder to think of the short- and long-term results that the council's cruel, expensive and unnecessary actions will have. I remind you that children as well as plants, birds and animals are to be found in the Six Dials area.

I am utterly disgusted by the council's behaviour and have realised that the council's 'Greener City Campaign' is nothing but a farce, an immoral and squanderous public relations exercise.

Paul was tempted to sign himself *Concerned Council Tax Payer*, but he signed *Paul Cloud* instead.

Dear Sir,

I am a council worker and don't want you killing birds in a car park. You will lose the votes on it.

Paul and Lucy advised Gilbert to remain anonymous in case he lost his job. Lucy wrote *Dear Madam or Sir*, then she drew a man in a spacesuit with a butterfly net and a gun, and made a shopping list.

Paul posted two of the letters that evening on his way to a talk on urban apiarists which he'd arranged at the Badger Centre. A week later a man who'd recently exchanged his wacky red-rimmed glasses for a pair of frameless oval ones read the letters to his secretary who was called Delilah. She stood no nonsense, but moved by her devotion to the city, the council, the voters and the environment, she dropped the letters into a bottle bank on her way to lunch.

Gilbert stayed for lunch at the Bluebird. He enjoyed his potato salad and his first ever garlic bread, but disliked the brown pastry on the spinach and feta pasty. He wasn't a great fan of cranberry juice either. He liked the carrot cake and the hazelnut ice cream. He declined coffee, but had tea with three again. Paul didn't charge him. Finally, Gilbert left. He had to hurry to make it to the last sitting, 2.30 p.m. at the canteen.

As the door closed behind him Lucy growled, 'What the hell do you think you're doing?'

'What?' Paul couldn't see anything wrong. He looked down at the table he was wiping. Did she mean his cleaning technique?

'You can't just dangle intimacy and friendship in front of people like that, and then have to snatch it away. He'll never leave us alone now.'

'I liked him. He was really interested in the goldfinches.'

'He's a nutter. Anyone can see that. He lives in that dreadful hotel!'

'I thought this was a café for everybody. Why shouldn't he come here? I thought you wanted some more business.'

'He didn't pay.'

'A loss leader, Lucy,' said Paul. 'Like the cheap bread in supermarkets.' Paul hated conflict. He tried to make her smile. 'He wasn't that crazy, and he ate loads, he really liked your cooking. Anyway, he probably won't come back.'

'Good,' said Lucy.

'But he might bring his friends,' said Paul.

'Great. All stinking of bins and damp.'

But Gilbert never did get into the habit of paying. He looked on Paul and Lucy as his new-found friends. He would come to the café every day after his rounds and talk to them while they worked. Then he'd look mournfully at the food. In the end they'd offer him something. He'd eat a great deal and then say, 'You really must let me give you something for this,' and before they could reply he'd slide 50p or occasionally a pound coin across the counter at them. If it was Lucy she'd say, 'Oh, thank you, Gilbert,' and put it in her pocket, as though it wasn't worth putting in the till. If it was Paul he'd put it in the Cats' Protection League collection tin. Abigail refused to talk to him. She stayed in the kitchen when he was there. She thought he was creepy and shouted, 'It's him! It's him!' at every police photofit she saw in the papers. Gilbert would sit in the café for hours. He'd look longingly at cakes and the urn, and tap his fingers against his mug when it was empty. He often told them that he was so pleased to have them as friends. He tried to help. He cleared tables and wiped them in great soapy swirls so that they'd need rinsing and drying afterwards. They couldn't tell him to leave. There was nothing they could do.

15

Sometimes at night Lucy turned into a Chagall woman. She flew around the flat, downstairs into the café, and around the kitchen. She could see the dirty tops of the cupboards and dust on the door frames. She circled the paper-moon lampshades and floated above tables. Sometimes Fennel caught a claw in Lucy's nightdress and jumped up for a ride. The ceiling was covered by a thin film of oil and cigarette tar. Paul's huge workman's boots were by the back door, their tongues lolling out in repose: dried mud was flaking and chunking on to the mat.

Sometimes Lucy wanted to fly out through the top half of a sash window, out into the beautiful night; but somehow she didn't, and she always woke up back in bed. Often when she woke she was thinking about the pond.

The pond embodied everything that Lucy thought was wrong with her life. When the environmental health officer gave them their first certificate he tut-tutted at it. It was too near the kitchen window, he said. Paul couldn't understand what the problem was. What were they worried about? Malaria?

'Oh, stagnant water, diseases, you know . . .' Lucy explained.

'I don't know,' said Paul. But they were told that if they wanted to put tables outside, the pond would have to go, and that new European legislation was coming in which governed the proximity of ponds to food preparation areas. (This was according to Paul's dad who was an expert on new European legislation that was coming in.)

'Safer for frogs in France,' Lucy said.

The pond would have dried up each summer, but Mr Snooke had ensured its survival by tipping saucepans of water into it. The water had sloshed down the front of his trousers and he'd heard the neighbours laughing at him. He had trudged backwards and forwards between the pond and the kitchen with his unwashed pale blue enamel pan, a hopeless contestant in a qualifying heat of a regional *It's a Knockout* that would never be screened. It hadn't occurred to him that the pondlife might not appreciate the fragments of coley and boil-in-the-bag cod in butter sauce which had burst from their plastic and were tipped into the pond with the tepid tap water.

Paul, of course, knew that it was wrong to put tap water into a pond and resolved to buy a butt to collect rainwater. He had seen one with a special attachment to connect it with a downpipe. £49.95 seemed a bit steep though, when the café was barely breaking even, but meanwhile, the dry weather continued and the pond was getting shallower and shallower.

'What if we put Highland Spring into it?' Lucy asked.

And then the last of the fish was discovered slashed and floating. The claw of suspicion pointed to Fennel.

The pond dried, the liner cracked. The frogs seemed to have hopped away and the irises wilted and died.

'Brown flags of our indecision and failure,' Lucy told Paul.

'Hmm,' he said, and looked away.

'At least we can fill it in now,' she added.

'But in the spring the frogs will come back here to spawn and find it gone.'

'It must happen in nature.'

'Lucy!'

Lucy caught herself thinking, Perhaps we'll have moved by the spring.

16

Paul used the *Thompson and Morgan* seed catalogue to get to sleep. A soft lawn of tranquillity grew from the shiny pages and enfolded him. As he read from abutilon to zinnia, from artichokes to zucchini, he saw the Bluebird's garden, and Giverny came to Southampton. He saw Lucy and himself sitting in faded green deckchairs drinking Pimms, or home-made lemonade, or pastis; ginger beer perhaps. There were sections on Chinese vegetables and herbs, pages and pages of tomatoes, gluts of cucumbers, more than a hill of beans. He was wearing a white cotton hat and listening to the cricket. A butterfly settled for a moment on Lucy's hot, tanned arm. Her skin smelled like snapdragons, like popcorn. Fennel stretched out on the tiles. He added 'nepeta' to his mental order form.

The Bluebird's garden had a fine crop of willowherb. Anonymous enemies threw used condoms over the wall. Paul sometimes found dirty nappies – disposable, ha! – and had to put them in carrier bags and dump them in their trade waste bin. In the flower beds were lumps of strange concretey stuff and broken bricks, but they had the original terracotta rope border edges. Nasturtiums thrived in the dusty earth. He was growing basil, parsley, chives, sweet marjoram, apple mint and lemon thyme for the café. He wouldn't mention the condoms or the nappies. There was a successful crop of purple sage, but Lucy wasn't sure what to do with it all.

Green fingers ran in Paul's family. Maggie Cloud's father was a champion pumpkin grower. Paul's earliest memories were of the pumpkins; being weighed in the balance against the year's finest (the pumpkin always winning), riding in the wheel-barrow, the terrible time when he'd thought that pumpkins bounced like space-hoppers, afternoons watering and weeding. Grandpa's name was engraved on the Pumpkin Trophy for twenty-two years in a neatly hoed row. When he died the village horticultural society brought wreaths of fruit and vegetables, as well as flowers.

The pumpkin-coloured banner outside the Sikh temple made Paul think of his grandfather. Perhaps they could have a PumpkinFest at the café. They could host an exhibition about The Role of the Pumpkin in Art, Architecture and Culture. He thought of banners, minarets, Hallowe'en, drinking vessels . . . he must discuss it with Lucy.

It was a Bank Holiday Monday and the café was closed. Paul was in the garden, sitting in a plastic chair which had once been white, but which Lucy had painted blue with paint that cost more than the chair itself. She had seen it done on *Home Front in the Garden*. He was listening to the cricket but every so often his ears flipped channels and he heard the sounds of B. J. Coles Funfair music thumping across from the Common. He hoped that the Badger Centre creatures wouldn't be upset. Fennel jumped up on to his lap and butted him with her warm, furry, precious head. Paul was having an almost perfect afternoon. Upstairs Fred and Ginger had been dancing cheek to cheek. Now they were in a snowstorm. Lucy was lying on the sofa and thinking, 'Huh. This is a fine romance.'

And when the credits rolled, she vowed to make a bit more

effort with Paul, to let him know that she loved him, to put some romance back into their relationship.

'Tulle, sequins and silhouettes are required,' she told herself. Perhaps she did need some more clothes. She wished that Paul liked to dance. She switched off the TV and went out into the garden.

'Paul,' she said. He held up a hand, gesturing silence.

'He runs up . . . blah blah blah . . . bowls . . . and he's out!' said the radio.

'Yes!' shouted Paul.

'Paul . . .' said Lucy.

'Bowled,' he told her, 'fifty-three for four. What?'

'I thought we might go out somewhere; the cinema, or out to dinner.'

'OK,' he said. 'After the cricket. You can choose where.'

'Decide where, you mean. Sort it all out . . .' she snapped, thinking that he couldn't be bothered. 'Aren't you interested? I want to go somewhere lovely, get dressed up.'

'Fine with me,' he said, and reached to turn the radio up.

Paul had been in the bath for fifty-four minutes. His watch was propped on top of the loo, but without his glasses he couldn't see its misted-over face. He had been doing the crossword but it was now too damp to be safely written on. He had two clues to go. He thought that he might even send it in, but he didn't want a leatherbound dictionary. He already had *Chambers*, the first shot in an exchange of fat reference books. The progress of their relationship was plotted in non-fiction along the bottom shelf of the bookcase. *Chambers, Roget's Thesaurus, The Times Atlas of the World, Atlas of the Stars, The Penguin Dictionary of Quotations,* and its brother, *Modern Quotations*. *British Flora and Fauna*. Claudia Roden's *The Food of Italy*, which was given special status.

Paul was thinking about Lucy and about their sex life. It had its moments but they never seemed to be able to sustain the good phases for more than a week or so. Peaks and troughs. They never seemed to talk about it. He wouldn't have minded, but Lucy would probably have been embarrassed.

Lucy wouldn't have expected Paul to want to talk about it. He was such a shrugger. She would also have been worried about saying something hurtful. She knew that she did have a problem with sex. She often seemed to lose the thread. She was easily distracted; a creak too many of the springs, a glimpse of something over Paul's shoulder, new ideas about other things swimming into her mind. Paul didn't know that some of her best recipes had come to her during their lovemaking. Worst of all, funny things often occurred to her. A few giggles could be disguised, but Paul didn't know that Lucy often had to suppress the urge to shout: 'Stop! Stop! From here you look like Michael Portillo!'

17

'It's her. From the *News*,' Lucy hissed at Paul.

'Who?'

'Her. In the pinky-red jacket and red glasses. She's from the *News*. She might be reviewing us. I recognise the glasses from her picture. I thought they were just using an old photo. She's called Sue Sholing, except she spells it S O O.'

'Like in Sooty,' said Paul, and they sniggered.

'What did they order?'

Paul was being the waiter that day.

'Chef's salad, fries, aubergine ravioli,' he said, consulting the pad.

'That should be all right then, I'll make them extra large ones. Do you mind if I use those artichoke hearts your mum brought us, that jar from France?'

This was a big sacrifice. Artichokes, hearts of palm and leeks and those French *carottes râpées* were Lucy's favourite foods.

'I don't mind. Thought we'd eaten them already,' said Paul.

The woman with the tight grey curls was Soo Sholing's mum. She was proud of her daughter and chuffed to be the My Companion in the review. She couldn't wait to show it to her friends, and she'd been thinking of lots of comments to make for Susan (as she still thought of her) to put in the paper. Things like 'a little dry', and 'slow on the palate', and 'over-seasoned'. Her friends must be thinking that Susan would end up as famous as that Jilly Goolden on *Food and Drink*. But anyone else

71

who took a good look at the pair of them tucking into their lunch, dabbing at greasy pink lips with Lucy's soft blue napkins, gripping their knives and forks with big, veiny, manicured hands, sniffing at the sauce with identical turned-up noses about which they were similarly vain, could see that Soo was turning into her mother, and that all the fuchsia-coloured jackets in the world couldn't save her.

'Do you think she'll write something horrible?' Lucy asked Paul.

'I don't like her jacket . . . but I suppose she might still be nice,' said Paul.

'I think she's a big cheese on the *News*. I'll talk to her when she asks for the bill.'

Half an hour later: 'Compliments of the house,' said Lucy, putting down a wooden disc tray bearing two pretty blue-and-white cups of coffee and a jug of cream and Lucy's own sugar bowl with its pattern of daisies. She'd decided against using her granny's sugar tongs, Soo Sholing might be light-fingered. Lucy remembered her granny telling her that if a member of the royal family admired anything the owner was expected to give it to them. Perhaps this rule applied to restaurant critics from provincial newspapers too. Lucy didn't want to chance it.

'Oh, thank you,' said Soo.

'I did recognise you,' said Lucy. 'I'm Lucy, the chef.'

'It's a very nice café, Lucy. Very homely.'

Lucy had always thought that 'homely' was an insult. Anne of Green Gables had always hated being called 'homely'. Perhaps it was a compliment for cafés.

'The rolls were lovely.'

'Oh. Thank you. My own recipe. The herbs are home-grown.'

'Very nice ravioli,' Soo's mum said. 'A lovely finish on the palate.'

'Thank you. My own recipe too.'

'You should write them down,' said Soo.

'I do. I have. I've got a bulging notebook. I love inventing things, changing them, adapting them. I always have.'

'Have you been cooking for a long time?' Soo asked, reaching for her notebook.

'Ever since I could hold a wooden spoon.' Lucy had been planning that line for a long time. It had been destined for the *Independent on Sunday*. 'I taught myself, well, with my mum's help, but I haven't been to catering college or anything. I came to Southampton to study English, and I just stayed here and opened the Bluebird.'

'Can I take a menu?' Soo asked.

'Please do, and come back soon.'

'I will,' said Soo, although she didn't really look the Bluebird type.

'Yes, we will,' said Soo's mum. Lucy guided them towards the door.

'I wouldn't usually say this,' said Soo, 'but you could try sending me a recipe or two for the Women's Page. I don't promise to use it, but we might. Put in some background. You said you did English. You know, when you first made the dish, where to shop, calories and so on . . .'

'Oh, I'd love to!' Lucy gushed.

'Well, here's my card.'

'Thank you!'

'This could really be something,' Lucy told Paul and Abigail. 'I might even get my own Cook's Column. I'll be a celebrity chef.'

'Well, Delia Smith started out in *Swap Shop*,' said Abigail.

The next week the Bluebird was reviewed in the *News*.

The Bluebird Café, 105 Bevois Valley Road

Lucy Brookes, the charming young proprietress of the Bluebird Café, says she has been cooking ever since she could hold a wooden spoon. The menu, prettily illustrated with birds and flowers, features many of her own creations. Lucy came to Southampton as a student and liked it so much that she stayed! Situated in what some people might call one of the city's seedier districts, the Bluebird is a little oasis of sophisticated home cooking at reasonable prices. Meat-eaters beware though, it's all vegetarian! There are about a dozen tables painted in pastel shades with old-fashioned chairs and a mural of birds and clouds. Portions are generous.

We enjoyed the complimentary rolls, which were freshly baked that day and flavoured with home-grown herbs, and the big helping of good old-fashioned thick-cut fries. My companion's aubergine ravioli were pretty parcels, fragrant with basil and that sort of thing, swimming in a classic Italian tomato sauce with a generous sprinkling of freshly grated Parmesan cheese. I munched my way through the chef's salad, and was impressed by the generous quantities of pricier ingredients such as artichoke hearts, asparagus points, olives, and by the many brightly coloured leaves.

My blackcurrant sorbet was delicious, velvety and smooth, and my companion's Inca pie was chocolate heaven. It certainly filled her up! Our bill with a bottle of mineral water came to £15.95. A real treat and quite a bargain too.

The Bluebird Café is open from 11 a.m. to 9 p.m., Monday to Saturday.

'It's a rave! Look, Paul!' Lucy waved it at him. She made copies to send to her relatives and to her friend Vicks and other people she wanted to impress.

'Do you think it would be tacky to put copies inside Christmas cards?' she asked Paul.

'Yes.'

They framed a copy and put it up in the window. Business did pick up.

'*Southampton News* readers can be your new target diners,' sniggered Abigail. 'You can be a stop-off on the coach excursions.'

Lucy stayed up late that night, looking through her recipe notebooks, writing her first column for Soo Sholing's Women's Page.

18

'I 'm just nipping to Vir and Vir for some Felix,' said Lucy.
'OK.'

John Vir was alone in the shop. He was bent over a huge box of packets of nuts. Lucy saw the Cash and Carry price on the outside.

'Wow! Where'd you get it that cheap?'

'Cash and Carry, near Basingstoke.'

'That's loads cheaper than the Wholefood Co-op we use.'

'Well, it would be, wouldn't it?' said John Vir.

'I don't use cashew nuts much because of the prices.'

'Oh, this one's good. Cheap prices. They have pistachios, peanuts, spices, everything. You give me a list if you like . . .' he offered.

'It sounds wonderful. But I don't want to put you to any trouble. You don't have a price list or anything, do you?'

'You could get your rice and yoghurt there too. Why not come with me and see yourself?' he said.

'That would be lovely,' Lucy said. 'I mean, very useful for the café. Paul will be pleased.'

'I'm going on Wednesday. How about four?'

She walked back to the Bluebird with a can of Felix in each hand.

'Paul,' she said, 'I'm going up to this really cheap, interesting Cash and Carry with the people from Vir's. Cheap nuts, rice, loads of things. Isn't that nice of them?'

'Yeah. Did you get any samosas?'

'Just catfood.'

John Vir called for Lucy at exactly four o'clock. She had been about to walk round to the shop to see if he had remembered their arrangement, when suddenly he was there in the doorway. His van, a strange, dolphinish-green, was parked outside.

'Oh God,' she thought, 'I can't think of anything to say.' She wished that she'd listed a few conversational topics on her cuff for easy reference. Then there she was, sliding on to the leatherette seat, belted in next to him, and his van was lumbering up The Avenue, the A33, towards the motorway. Lucy loved The Avenue, it was so impressively tree-lined and the views of Southampton Common were beautiful. She loved walking up it, driving up it, riding up it in a van. It made her think of Judy Garland dressed as a tramp with a smudge on her nose, a broken hat, and a blacked-out tooth. She could remember all the words. It had been her moment of glory as a Young Stager, singing 'We're a Couple of Swells' with her friend Sally, before some blonde Miss Piggy ballet-type had danced to 'Evergreen'.

'What are you humming?' asked John Vir.

'Was I?' Lucy had thought the song was just playing in her head. Now she was embarrassed. 'Can we have the radio on?'

He switched it on. It crackled. Lucy hated trying to tune in other people's car radios. It was impossible. John Vir found Radio Solent.

'And in *Scene South* today we have a special report on Southampton's Fluoridation Debate.'

'Oh, honestly,' said Lucy.

'Blah blah blah,' said John. He twisted the dial and the van was filled with music and sunlight. It was 'Natural Woman'. Lucy had to stare out the window in embarrassment. The light from the sun streamed through the clouds in golden shafts. As a child Lucy had thought that these were the ladders for dead people to go up to heaven, and for the angels to come down to earth. The road glistened ahead of them. John Vir pulled down his sun-shield, dazzled.

'So what are you looking for?' he asked.

'Oh God, well,' said Lucy, thinking that he meant in life.

'I get the same stuff every week. Customers just want the same. Crisps, nuts, spices, flour, oils.'

They waltzed around the Cash and Carry together, loading their trolleys. When Lucy reached the checkout she realised that she was spending much more than she'd planned; but John Vir's bill was five times the size of hers. She fumbled in her bag for more money, pulling out her salsa-stained chequebook with its embarrassing NatWest otters and weasels. John Vir pulled a wad of crisp twenties out of his back pocket. He had a little gilt money clip, and peeled off thirty notes.

They loaded up the van. The space between the two rows of back seats was filled with boxes and sacks, on the top was a layer of packets of crisps, all the Monster Munch and Hula Hoops and Skips and everything that his customers would want in the next week.

'Looks quite comfortable,' joked Lucy, as they put the last few twelve-packs on top.

He pictured them lying there. He had to stop himself from taking her and pushing her down on to that soft bed of packets. He was that close.

19

J ohn Vir unloaded her boxes from the back of the van and stacked them up in the doorway of the Bluebird.

'I can bring them inside for you,' he offered.

'No, they're fine here, but' – she realised that he had never, ever been inside the café before – 'if you'd like a cup of tea . . .' then Paul appeared and began to carry the boxes inside.

'Thanks,' he said. 'See you.' John Vir turned and left.

'Paul!' she said, annoyed. 'I was going to ask him, he might have wanted to come in. What's that?'

Somebody had shoved a note through the door.

'I thought I might have heard someone. I was upstairs. There weren't any customers, so I locked up . . . There might have been someone knocking.'

'But you didn't think to answer.'

'Not really.'

She unfolded the note, her face crumpled.

'CAT UNDER PLANT IN FRONT GARDEN'.

She was biting her lip. Fennel.

'What's wrong?'

She handed him the note.

'Stay here,' said Paul, but of course they went together. Lucy thought, 'This is my punishment,' and then hated herself for thinking about John Vir and not Fennel. There was a bulky-looking Safeway's bag poking out from under the morning glory.

'I can't look,' thought Lucy, but of course she would have to. She had lost a cat before. She remembered the damp fur that had lost its shine, the beloved body gone stiff, paws frozen.

Paul knelt and gently parted the tangle of fronds. Blue trumpets sounded a silent blast. There was a copy of the *Next Directory* inside the bag. A CATalogue.

Lucy looked for something to order Fennel to show her how much she was loved, perhaps a navy blazer or a black jumper to lie on, some curtains to rip or an armchair to scratch.

'What about a pair of tights to catch her claws in?' Paul suggested.

'An armchair or a sofa would be better. Up to £1,000 instant credit.'

'Hmm.'

20

When Lucy lay in bed, trying to get to sleep, Gilbert's voice would ring in her ears.

'Would you like me to wipe down the tables, Lucy? It's no trouble . . .' and 'Would you like me to fill up the salt pots, Lucy? It's no trouble. I could do the pepper pots too . . .' and 'Would you like me to wipe down the counter for you, Lucy? It's no trouble.' It drove her crazy that he always used her name in such a ponderous way. She had also noticed, and it was a Southampton thing, that tables and counters were always wiped *down*, things fried *up*, or dusted *off*. In Southampton nothing was just plain *done*. Perhaps she had been here for too long.

She would lie for what seemed like hours watching light beams from passing cars sweep around the ceiling. Paul usually seemed to be asleep, or to be doing a pretty good impression of someone being asleep. Sometimes she would whisper, 'Paul – Paul – are you asleep?' and sometimes when she did this he was instantly awake and would hold her. When he didn't answer she would sometimes kiss him on the shoulder blade or place one of her hands on his thigh and beam him messages of love, or at least kind thoughts and good will.

John Vir had decided to change his life. He usually did at around 11.30 on Sunday evenings, but this time he really meant it. He always really meant it, but this time he really did mean it. He was going to win Lucy. He would do whatever it took. She was going to be his. He thought of her soft hair, her sweet nose, her cool, slim hands, the way her collarbone jutted out when she shrugged, her feet in those floppy cotton shoes she always wore. What was it they called them? Escargots. Something like that. Perhaps he could get some at the Cash and Carry, and sell them in the shop. She might try them on. He could picture her slipping them on and off.

Lucy was woken by *Farming Today*. She switched it off. She stared at the ceiling and made meticulous, itemised lists in her head. At 6.43 she got out of bed. At 7 a.m. Fennel was eating Arthur's Meaty Chunks With Game. At 7.04 a cup of tea was placed beside Paul's sleeping head, where it could be discovered at 8.30 a.m. She had a bath and then cleaned the bathroom with special attention to the algae that had grown in the overflow of the basin. The clogged nozzle of Paul's shaving foam was rinsed, the mirror was wiped, the flannels folded neatly, new soap was unwrapped, the towels were folded. Lucy could never decide whether flowers in the bathroom were naff or not, somehow akin to M&S peach-scented toiletries. The flat was hoovered, dusted, blitzed! The geraniums were dead-headed, the windowsills wiped. Would she have time to clean the windows? No! No! But she did wipe the milk shelf in the fridge. Paul emerged at 8.45, made toast, made crumbs, was banned from mucking up the bathroom and told to do the potatoes. They made moussaka and salad and took a café apple pie out of the freezer. The hideous, cheese-encrusted sandwich toaster was hidden at the back of a cupboard. Paul put on a pot of coffee. At 11.45, right on schedule and half an hour early, his parents arrived.

'I'm sorry the place is in such a mess,' said Lucy.

'Oh, that's all right, dear,' said Maggie Cloud. 'We don't expect you to go to any trouble.'

They were sitting down to lunch. Whatever she did, whatever she and Paul cooked, or even if they were abroad or in a restaurant, Paul's family always spent these special or family celebration meals discussing other meals they had eaten.

'Remember those king prawns we had in Portugal . . .'

'At that little place with the farm implements on the ceiling . . .'

'And those stuffed trotters at that one with the double loos . . .'

'And where the waiter showed you your fish before it was cooked . . .'

'And remember when we had that wonderful chicken with lime . . .'

'It was lemon grass.'

'Oh yes, in that French-Thai place where they gave us those awful soggy sesame crackers . . .'

'And we weren't sure if she'd spilled something on them without realising it.'

'I think they'd stayed out in the sun too long – or we had – ha ha ha!'

It was a litany. Lucy had to dig her nails into her palms under the table. If she'd been at Malory Towers she'd have been stuffing her clean hanky into her mouth.

'Oh God, and when we went to America – the amount they eat is disgusting!' Paul's mother would say as she helped herself to a little more potato salad. 'At breakfast I'd say,

"But I just want eggs on toast with a little bacon and tomato." But they'd insist on bringing you this huge *platter*! And the cakes! The amount they eat is disgusting. They'd have a whole sponge cake to themselves. No wonder they are so obese as a nation.'

'Remember those steaks they gave us at that little taverna above Firenze? They just show them the flame!'

'Oh, and that asparagus there, and that bread!'

'Remember those watermelon ice creams we had in Geneva . . .' And they were off again. They had eaten the whole of Europe.

The first time Lucy met the Clouds, she thought, My God. Perhaps I have completely the wrong idea about him. Paul became subtly different; but she got used to it, and saw the ways in which he was a different sort of Cloud and had detached himself from his parents. He managed not to carry a thermos of coffee on all car journeys or clean his shoes *every* Sunday night. He recklessly patted strange cats.

After lunch, Paul's parents visited Vir and Vir to stock up on spices, curry paste and cheap peppercorns.

'So much cheaper than Sainsbury's,' said Maggie. Her real name was Magnolia.

'Why on earth doesn't she insist on Magnolia?' Lucy wondered as she peeled off her Marigolds. She'd just done all of the clearing up by herself, having decided to give the family outing to Vir and Vir a miss.

'I do go there every day,' she told them.

The Clouds bought themselves a large sack of meat samosas

and heated them up under the grill while Lucy dried the last of the lunch things. Then they all drove to the New Forest to visit a deer sanctuary.

'I'm thinking of joining a contemplative order,' Lucy told Paul as they queued to get on to the wooden deer-viewing platform.

'Me too,' said Paul.

'Oh, look! There's a whole flock of them over there!' cried Maggie Cloud.

'Not a flock, a herd!' James corrected her. He had a keen interest in collective nouns. Everyone ignored him, including the deer who were sleeping in the sun or audibly grazing, oblivious to the fact that every middle-class child in Hampshire had come to visit them.

On the way home they stopped in Lyndhurst so that James could buy a tub of New Forest Venison Pâté. Lucy bought a postcard of some dreary New Forest ponies standing around looking cold.

When at last they left, Maggie squeezed Lucy's hand and said, 'It's so lovely to have you coming into the family.'

Lucy nearly said: 'WHAT?' but instead she said: 'Oh, thank you,' and kissed Maggie on the cheek. When they'd gone she asked Paul what 'coming into the family' might mean.

'She must be expecting us to get married,' he said. 'She asked me if we were thinking about it.'

'Oh?'

'I said we might think about it.'

'Might we?'

'Oh, Lucy, you know I'd like to marry you.'

She said nothing. Paul opened a can of lager.

'Give us a swig,' said Lucy. 'There wouldn't be meat on the menu at the reception.'

'Reception?'

And then the phone rang.

A 'thank you for a nice day' present from Maggie Cloud arrived in the post. It was a special roly thing for massaging tired feet. It looked like a medieval torture implement, and was made of wood from sustainable forests. Lucy was pleased with it, but Paul said, 'Things like this don't need to exist. There should be special licences that people have to obtain before they can go making any more crap. There's too much *stuff* in the world already. People shouldn't be able to manufacture something unless they can prove that it is really necessary, that it will add to the sum of global happiness and well-being.'

There was no more talk of weddings for quite some time.

That night, in the privacy of their own bed, back home in Sussex, Maggie Cloud said: 'I really do like Lucy, but I must say that for someone who runs a restaurant, or would you call it a café, or a bistro, she doesn't seem very interested in food.'

'They call it a café,' her husband told her.

21

The Bluebird Café was the only shop in the street that lacked a security grille. John Vir was raising his, but Lucy and Paul were asleep and didn't hear. It had been a heavy night. The Bluebird had been full. A party of women with eating disorders had booked for five but turned up with twelve. The debut of Lucy's pecan pie had been a great success. As the last compulsive eater had cycled whistling into the night, Paul and Lucy had melted like toffee into each other's arms. They had made a profit, and consequently the Bluebird wasn't going to open until at least noon the next day.

John Vir wondered where his brother had got to. He hadn't seen him for weeks. Two paper boys were approaching. He was thankful that so few of the locals wanted their papers delivered. He paid a generous weekly wage, but it was getting increasingly difficult to find willing children. He sometimes had to deliver the papers himself. His kids would never have agreed to get up so early, or to be seen dead doing something like that. Now he knew how the grey cotton straps dug into the paper boys' shoulders, and how those huge fluorescent bags thudded on to their thighs with every step.

The large orange notice asking for paper boys or girls or even (this desperate) active pensioners brought few enquiries. He wondered if any of the other posters and flyers that he agreed to display in the window, advertising things like Green Party meetings, jumble sales, Crèche Workers Wanted For Punjabi Women's Group, Islamic Students' Day of Prayer, had any more luck.

John Vir's spirits plummeted whenever he found a left-behind shopping list on the counter or the floor, or in a basket. He'd hated lists ever since his wife had left him and he'd found the one she'd made. On one side was:

underwear
slipper
housecoat
brush
passport
cloths
maked up
money
nail files

On the other side were two columns, For and Against. He had seen that Against was against staying with him. There was also a name, Raj, and a phone number. Who was Raj? They knew lots of Rajes. He saw that the number wasn't local. He dialled it.

'Good morning! You're through to *This Morning* and Dr Raj Persaud. Please hold. Your call is being held in a queuing system and one of our operators will talk to you soon.' But an operator didn't. It was the afternoon and the show was over. The line went dead. As he listened to the monotone of nothing he studied her lists. For and Against.

For	*Against*
Quite tall	Dirty feet
Opens pickle jars	Doesn't take notice
	Doesn't help with kids
	No ambition
	Lazy
	Won't wash van
	Not romantic
	Not firm
	Gives tic

His heart had broken, not just because she had left him, but because she had decided to do so on a daytime TV phone-in, probably in front of five million viewers, while he was downstairs in the shop bundling up the *News* from yesterday.

22

When Lucy put plates in front of customers she stared at their hands. She had realised that you could tell how old people were by their hands, the elasticity of the skin, the wrinkliness, the faded or yellowed nails. She was keeping an eye on her own and thought that she could detect the first signs of decay, a certain greyness about the knuckles, a shininess of the skin over the third phalange. She was so busy spying on her hands that she failed to notice a rearguard action. And then one day, trying on some trousers and checking that her bum didn't look big, she saw that there were somebody else's elbows attached to her arms. She was turning into her old RE teacher, Miss Dowling, starting with the elbows. She wondered if there was a diet to save elbows, or the backs of knees, which also worried her. She thought that she might have some invisible varicose veins. She wouldn't talk to Paul about it. She didn't want to tarnish the image he had of her. She remembered reading somewhere that you should sit with your elbows in lemon halves for half an hour every week. She could attach the lemons with Sellotape and carry on cooking. She decided to write a book, *How to Firm Your Elbows and Rid Yourself of Invisible Varicose Veins*. Daytime TV beckoned. She was expounding it to Abigail, but Abigail wasn't listening. She was staring out of the café window.

'That's Chris Packham! Look!'

'Who?' Lucy asked, staring at the wrong person.

'Chris Packham from the *Really Wild Show*!'

'Oh, is he famous?'

'There's Paul, showing him something. Birds or something.'

'He's quite good-looking, isn't he?'

'Who, Paul? I've always thought so.'

'Chris Packham! Paul too, of course . . . Let's go and see what they're looking at.'

'And get his autograph.'

There were waxwings in the trees along Bevois Valley, blown in by a north-easterly. They were up in the sycamore trees speaking Swedish and maybe thinking of home where their name was Silky Tail. Paul and Chris Packham stood side by side staring at them intently through binoculars. Paul's binoculars had been borrowed eight years ago from his parents' neighbours, Jackie and Tim Gibson-Down. Sometimes he remembered this and thought about giving them back the next time he visited his parents, but then he always forgot again. Paul wasn't thinking about this, he was wondering how the birds knew to come to Bevois Valley, Southampton. How did they know that behind the closed-down army surplus store, the down-at-heel cobbler, the catering equipment company where nobody could ever possibly buy anything, was an avenue of rowans hung with green orbs of mistletoe?

After three days all of the rowan and mistletoe berries were gone. Chris Packham left too, but gave the café a signed *Really Wild Show* Poster. Paul discovered that they had somehow managed to exchange binoculars. He must tell the Gibson-Downs. Perhaps they'd think it was funny.

23

I s there a moment of falling in love? A tipping of the balance? A stepping across the stream? A switching on of a light? For Abigail there was.

They'd been on the same courses. She'd sneered at his name – Teague – honestly! She'd thought him a bit of a poseur and a know-all. He swotted for tutorials. He'd spent two years digging in northern Germany; he'd gone for his gap year and they'd asked him to stay. He hobnobbed with the junior lecturers. He was potentially quite hateful, but also good-looking. He was tall and dark and wore a piratical bandanna around his wiry curls. He wore very long shorts, short longs as she came to think of them, from May to October, and never any socks. He had greeny-brown eyes, a very wide smiley mouth, long limbs. Unlike most of the boys on the course, he didn't look medieval, he looked rakish. So Abigail, as a matter of principle, decided not to be charmed by him, or at least not to appear to be charmed by him.

Then one day they were digging in one of the city vaults, excavating a medieval wine cellar, when Teague found a buckle. It was verdigris green, about two inches square with a tiny pin. It lay in his palm, and he ran his finger around its edges, cupped his hand and cradled it, safe, safe, safe. It was the look of pure pleasure at his find that did it. She was bowled over, smitten.

*   *   *

Lucy was washing up and thinking, 'At what point do you give up? At what point do you capitulate and decide that you are going to be ordinary? At what point do you *settle* for things and think, "No, it hasn't got to be perfect"?'

That song was always punching out its melody in her head in time to eggs being beaten, tables wiped, her feet crossing and recrossing the kitchen floor, the rhythm of driving. 'It's got to be e e ee ee perfect.'

At what point did a person say to themselves: 'The creature who is my destiny will be hunched and porky . . .' Now, that was bigoted. But she couldn't give up yet. She was still waiting for the band to strike up, and to find herself whirling in silhouette, cheek to cheek. Was that special someone Paul? Well, yes, probably, most of the time. If she could disregard the dirty socks on the floor, the smell of mice on his clothes. Aha! So that was it, the first slip on the slippery slope.

24

The thick creamy envelope was decorated with a spray of lilac roses; a colour which Lucy had always hated and which Paul pointed out was quite unnatural for roses.

'But then roses today . . .' His voice trailed off.

'Spitting on the streets, elbowing past old folks to get to the front of bus queues. Too much money and freedom. Don't know the value of anything, especially good manners,' Lucy added.

The envelope was lined with tissue paper in a contrasting blue. 'Ouch,' said Lucy, as it gave her a vicious cut. 'Damn.' She sucked her finger and tasted blood, Body Shop cocoa butter lotion and onions.

Mr and Mrs Michael Pennington
Request the pleasure of your company
At the marriage of their daughter
Victoria Jane
to
Mr Angus Lennox Keen
At St Mary's Church, Reigate
On Saturday 26 June at 3.30 p.m.
And afterwards at
The Tythe Barn, Oxlease Lane
RSVP

'Oh God. Vicks is getting married to Angus Keen. How could she?'

Paul looked blank. 'What, that rugby player? Have we got to go?'

'Of course we've got to bloody go. She's one of my best friends.'

'You haven't seen her for ages.'

'So? We're very close. Well, we were once. And every one will be there.'

'Who?'

Lucy ignored him. 'But most importantly, what can I wear? . . . I wonder who the bridesmaids are.' She was relieved that she wasn't one, but wondered if she should feel hurt.

'Some small cousins, I expect,' said Paul. Vicks had been one of Lucy's best friends during their first year at university, but they'd drifted apart.

'Where's that *Next Directory*? I'll need a hat too.'

'Do I have to wear a special hat too?' Paul asked, aghast.

'You can wear your twitcher's hat.'

Paul laughed. It was a tweed cap that had been his grandfather's. It was so filthy that it provided excellent camouflage in bushes or muddy places.

'I wonder if she's pregnant or something. It's only six weeks away.'

'Ring her up,' said Paul.

'OK. Well, maybe I'll wait till after six. Everybody will be ringing now. I might go into town if you'll look after the café for me this afternoon. Tuesdays are never very busy. Just to look. I can always wear that blue dress.'

'You always look nice in that,' said Paul. Lucy had worn that blue dress to their graduation and to every smart occasion they'd been to since.

'Or maybe I could get something in Portswood Scope Shop,' she said.

Even Paul could see that a new dress was required. 'Here,' he said, taking £100, three days' profit, out of the till. 'Go and buy yourself something pretty.'

'I've always wanted someone to say that to me.'

'And I've always wanted to say it.'

'My God!' What was this? How could people be so blatantly acquisitive? It was Vicks and Angus Keen's wedding list from Peter Jones, Sloane Square.

'I think it must be what they call a Pay Party,' said Lucy. The wedding list had arrived by return of post when they RSVPed. 'Lime-and-turquoise madras check cushion covers. Gross. A Dualit toaster. Three sets of napkins. A £120 picnic hamper. I didn't know they went on picnics.'

'Have we got to buy something off this then?' Paul asked.

'Yes. You have to ring up and then post a cheque or something . . . plates, plates, plates. Platters, bowls, cereal bowls, pasta bowls, avocado bowls. Seven, eight, nine, ten- and twelve-inch cake tins. She doesn't even like cooking. Blue Denby mugs. I think those are compulsory.'

Paul didn't seem that interested, but she carried on anyway.

'Five Le Creuset saucepans. Five! A Le Creuset gratin dish, £38! Glasses . . . glasses. A £58 laundry basket . . . £34.95 bathroom scales. £38 kitchen clock. Four different chopping boards. Six sheets, three quilt covers, twelve pillow cases. Honestly!' She passed it to Paul.

'Here's ours,' he said. 'Strawberry huller. £2.85. Or egg cups, £8 for three. Do you think you can buy them separately? They can't really need all of this stuff.'

'Well, they are lawyers,' said Lucy.

'So?'

'Well, that might mean they need it all . . . or that they are rich enough to buy it themselves, I suppose.'

'Mmm.'

'We could get something together with Abigail and Teague,' Lucy suggested.

'Are they going?'

'I assume so. I hope so or we won't have anyone to talk to.'

'There's garden stuff too, Lucy. How about a terracotta planter? £8.99 to £34.99. We could get one of those. At that price they must be big.'

Lucy and Paul, Abigail and Teague were an hour early. They decided to wait in the Squirrel and Firkin which had once been the King's Head and was just around the corner from the church.

'I think we're among fellow guests,' said Lucy.

'Either that or it's a hats theme pub,' said Teague.

'Well, I hope we don't meet anyone we know,' said Paul.

'Isn't that a bit of the point of coming?' said Abigail.

'Surely we don't have to be sociable till after the ceremony?' he continued. 'I'll get the drinks. Two dry white wine and sodas, and two pints of Flowers,' he told the barman.

'Spritzers,' the barman corrected him.

'People wouldn't know what we meant if we asked for spritzers where we come from,' said Lucy.

'Southampton,' said Paul.

'You're not in Southampton now though, are you?' the barman replied with a menacing glint. They turned away.

'Are you allowed to drink beer at weddings, before the ceremony?' Lucy asked Paul, hoping that he wouldn't smell of it in the church, but then she saw him reach for the bowl of complimentary peanuts on the bar. All was lost. What with the perpetually crumpled knees of his trousers, even though that suit had just been dry-cleaned, and them not asking for 'spritzers' and her flat shoes and the ancient tapestry knitting bag that had seemed such a stylish alternative to a handbag back home in Southampton, and arriving in the café van, wondering if they'd be mistaken for the caterers, they were a pair of frumps, freaks, country bumpkins. A Couple of Swells. It made her smile into her glass. She felt in her bag for cough sweets to mask the peanuts, beer and wine.

'Lucy! You do look sweet!' Some bright red lips darted at her. 'And Paul!'

'Sara. Hi! We didn't know you were coming. I didn't know you were still in touch with Vicks.' (And I didn't think she liked you, Lucy thought.)

'Oh, look,' said Sara. 'There's Abigail and Teal. Are they still together?'

'Very much. They might go on a three-year dig in Yorkshire together.'

'Hi, Sara, how are you?' said Abigail. Sara, Abigail and Lucy had been in the same block of their hall of residence, but Sara and Abigail hadn't ever really hit it off. Sara was too keen on early-morning tennis for Abigail's liking; also her boyfriends gratuitously stole other people's food from the communal fridge.

'And this is Toby. Toby du Bois,' said Sara. They obviously should have heard of him. The men nodded at each other, all still silent.

'Toby and I met while I was still just a sub.'

'Subaltern, submarine, subwhat?' thought Paul.

'Oh. Have you managed to break into journalism then?' said Abigail, all innocence.

'I'm a staff reporter on the *Indie*. So's Toby.'

'Sports,' said Toby.

'You look sporty,' said Lucy, hoping he would take it as an insult.

'I row. And run, of course.'

'Of course,' said Lucy.

'He's really fit,' said Sara.

'And what do you do?' Toby du Bois asked them all and nobody in particular. Silence.

'These three are finishing PhDs,' said Lucy. 'I run a café.'

'Whereabouts? Would I have been there?'

'It's in Southampton,' said Lucy.

'I once caught a boat from Southampton. I was seven.'

'Oh.'

'We could go over to the church now. It's ten past three.'

'I'm just going to the loo,' said Abigail.

The bride wore a long ivory tulip, or perhaps an Easter lily, but with too much make-up. It looked like stage make-up in daylight, bright orange panstick with outlined eyes. She would look hot and startled in the photos. Would it ruin her day if someone suggested that she clean some of it off, or just ruin it retrospectively if they didn't and she found out when she saw the video? Lucy and Abigail decided to keep quiet. Paul didn't notice, he was watching a spider spinning a web across a stained-glass window of St Francis.

They mouthed the words to 'Love Divine, All Love Excelling', 'Jerusalem' and 'How Great Thou Art'. Odd choices, really. The vicar's address was innocuous. Lucy studied hats. How odd, she thought, that supposedly sane and sensible women would choose to put these expensive concoctions of straw, paper, feathers, net, ribbons and fripperies on their heads and then go out wearing them. Upturned baskets, disembowelled Easter eggs, how ridiculous and how touching that this collection of quite ordinary women should think their heads worthy of such adornment. Lucy's hat was blue silk with a wide brim, pinned up at the front with a creamy silk rose. By far the best, she thought, and not bad for £19.99. Abigail's was bright yellow straw with some papery poppies, daisies and cornflowers. The sort of hat that a donkey in a picture would wear.

The spider was now filling in the web with hexagons, no, duodecagons, what was the name for a shape with that many sides, Paul wondered. Then Lucy nudged him and everyone stood up and the grinning bride and groom were exiting to 'The Arrival of the Queen of Sheba'. Lucy seemed to be wiping her eyes. Paul put an arm around her and they waited to shuffle out into the churchyard for the photographs.

Bride and Groom. Bride and Groom and Bridesmaids. Bride and Groom and Bridesmaids and Best Man. Bride and Bride's mother. Bride's mother and grandparents and Bride and Groom. All Bride's family. All Groom's family. Bride and Groom and Groom's family. Friends from University Days. All the grandparents. All the children.

'What, will the line stretch out to the crack of doom?' hissed Abigail to Lucy. Lucy wished that she smoked and envied people who were flicking ash on to the eighteenth-century tombs which provided such convenient props. Even the bride's mother was getting impatient. A forty-eight-seater coach was running its engine, waiting to take the guests to the reception in a converted tythe barn twenty miles away.

'So this is how love and passion are meant to end up,' said Abigail as they piled on to the coach. 'Quick! Get the back seat!'

'But the service was lovely,' said Lucy. She saw that Teague was wearing muddy desert boots. Paul looked pretty smart in comparison.

'We should have brought a hip flask,' said Paul.

'I did. Here.' Teague had it inside his jacket.

'They assured me that the pigeons would be out of here!' The bride's mother was fuming. The tythe barn's resident pigeons had guanoed on the top table's tablecloth and flown off with some devils on horseback. It took three hours to get from the church to the watercress soup (conveniently served cold). Lucy realised that she had used the wrong spoon for her soup. She surreptitiously wiped it on her napkin and put it back with her pudding fork. It was all downhill from there.

'Did you know that seventy per cent of married couples met at other people's weddings?' Teague told her.

'Seventy per cent – no way!'

'Studies have been done.'

'No, that's ridiculous. Seventy per cent have *been* to *weddings* maybe.' They looked around the room and then at each other and then at Abigail and Paul who were laughing at something. The pigeons probably.

Finally, pretty little net bags of sugared almonds arrived on their plates.

'What the hell are these?' Teague picked his up as though it was an artefact, a find, and examined it.

'Sugared almonds,' Lucy told him. 'You're meant to keep it, or take it home anyway. Men don't always get them. A sort of going-home present, sort of good luck. They're called Bridal Flavours.'

'An amulet against getting hitched like this,' said Teague. 'Or a fertility symbol or offering, perhaps.'

Abigail looked sad. 'Well, some of it's lovely,' she said.

'This pink nylon net of sweets?' Teague was incredulous. 'Think of the waste of the world's resources. The unnecessary squandering. The petrol burned to get all of these people here. The money they've wasted on all of these never-to-be-worn-again hats and clothes, that stack of presents. That white dress she's wearing must have cost a few grand. And what for?'

'Actually, it was made by a Women's Fair Trade Co-operative in Central America and provided a year's income for a whole village,' said Abigail.

'Seventy per cent of the country's economy pivots on weddings,' said Lucy. 'Studies have been done. Didn't you know?'

'I don't suppose Teague and I'll be getting married like this,' Abigail's reflection told Lucy's as they washed their hands. There were little baskets of pot-pourri, peach and apricot, and dispensers of M&S hand lotion between each sink. Nobody nicked them. The speeches were over and the dancing had begun.

'We'd never be able to afford it. And I'd feel silly asking my parents if they'd pay for me to dress up as a cake. They thought they got me off their hands when I was eighteen.'

'I would quite like to get married though.'

'Mmm.'

'I don't know why.'

'Who said "Every woman looks like a bride in her slip"?' Lucy asked.

'E. M. Forster? Diana Vreeland?'

'That's "Pink is the navy blue of India", isn't it?' said Lucy.

'Was it the Duchess of Windsor? We'll just have to wear our petticoats anyway,' said Abigail, and they smiled at each other in the mirror.

'Mine's black tactel.'

'The very thing.'

25

John Vir's passion for Lucy was growing. He wanted to hold her tightly. He wanted to smooth that dark wing of hair back from her forehead. He wanted to run away with her, to run away from Gurpal and the boys, and his brother, the whole lot of them, the tick book and the van's dodgy suspension, the students buying frozen spinach to make vegetarian lasagne, when he had great fresh stuff, wilting by the box load, and braying at each other across the shop as though he and the family couldn't understand, the past-it fruit, and that tin of Tibet sandalwood talc that accused him and condemned him from its rusty island in the bathroom cabinet.

He wanted to start again with Lucy. They would have to go away somewhere. He longed for her. His longing nagged at him like toothache, like a wisdom tooth trying to break through. He thought that she must like him a bit . . . when they'd been to the Cash and Carry together . . . oh. But she was all tied up in that café. There was nothing for it. He would have to kill Paul.

He sat behind the shop counter and made a plan. He would push Paul into the freezer room and leave him there, then chuck him in the river when he was frozen. It would be so easy. He'd just wait until the next time Paul came in. He'd say: 'How are you, Paul? Have you seen these beans we have in?' He'd have them by the freezer door. When Paul bent to look at them he'd just shove him in and bolt the door. Nobody would hear him scream. Easy.

It was the perfect plan, until he realised that he'd got the idea from an episode of *The Bill* where some Indian brothers had burned the body of a rival in a tandoori oven. He'd be the prime suspect. He'd have to think again.

Meanwhile, he could try to see more of Lucy. The trips to the Cash and Carry could become regular. Perhaps she would come with him each time he went. He decided to ask.

'Lucy,' he said, when she came in the next morning for her paper. 'Lucy, perhaps you would like some more things from the Cash and Carry soon?'

'Oh, when are you going?'

'In the next few days.'

'We do need some things – rice, nuts, you know. If it wouldn't be any trouble.'

'Shall we go on Thursday then? About four o'clock?'

'Great,' said Lucy. Why was she blushing? Why was her hand shaking? On her way out she tripped on a pile of unsold *News*es.

'Oh God,' she said, 'I'm clumsy.' He rushed from behind the counter to help her up and knocked over a plastic tub of Rainbow Drops. It rolled off the counter and a confetti of the magic chocolate discs landed on her shoes and around her feet.

'Sorry, sorry,' he said, 'but you look good enough to eat.' They piled the Rainbow Drops back into the pot. Lucy realised later that he was still intending to sell them, dust and all, to the crowds of children who arrived in the shop less than sixty seconds after the infants school kicked out.

When Lucy got back to the Bluebird, Abigail was slicing aubergines for a terrine they had planned for the evening –

layers of fried aubergine with roasted peppers, basil and a cheesy mousse.

Lucy noticed a Rainbow Drop stuck to her sleeve. She prised it off and popped it into her mouth. Hundreds and thousands grazed her tongue and the roof of her mouth.

'I was thinking,' said Paul later that evening. 'You keep saying that you could do with some really good saucepans. Do you think that we should get married?'

Lucy's mouth fell open like a cartoon character's.

'What, us?'

'Well, we do love each other. We could have the reception here,' said Paul, as if that was an added bonus that would persuade her.

'And Gilbert could be the toastmaster. I don't think so.'

'Well, perhaps not,' said Paul. 'It was just a thought.'

'I'm going to the Cash and Carry with John Vir on Thursday,' said Lucy.

'Oh.'

'Would you help make a list?'

26

Lucy felt as though she was turning into someone else's mother; developing strong brawny arms from lifting pans, and mixing and kneading. Postcards arrived from friends travelling in Mexico and Cuba, or working in Australia, or worst of all from former best friends who were working in London. Purple ink from Tessa at drama school. 'Course hard but am getting very THIN and playing Ophelia next month. Why don't you ever come up? Having a lovely time. Wish you were here.'

'Do you?' thought Lucy. 'I haven't got your phone number.'

'I feel isolated,' she told Paul.

'What from?'

'Life.'

'Mmm . . . I don't think your beans are sprouting.'

The bean sprouter, an expensive plastic box, wasn't working. Bean sprouts had started to disgust her. Sliced celery looked like maggots. She avoided organic produce now, too many insects to save or kill. Would irradiation kill them? Or make them grow bigger perhaps? They'd hatch in the oven and crawl out of pies and pastries; armies, legions of insects with plastic indestructible bodies and cellophane wings.

'Oh, bean sprouts. What care I for bean sprouts?' said Lucy. But Paul had wandered away.

*   *   *

The next time Lucy saw John Vir he looked somehow different.

'How are you?' she asked, trying to see what the difference was.

'Fine, thank you, Lucy,' he said. 'My sister, Shreela, is staying. She's a very good cook.'

He looked different because he looked fatter, heavier, but, to Lucy, in a good way, not flabby, more weighty.

'Look.' (Why was she smiling at him like that?) 'Why don't you and your boyfriend come for dinner one night?' It was an outrageous thing to ask. He didn't ask people to dinner! He never had visitors now except family, or the children's friends. He hadn't even discussed it with Shreela. She'd have to help him. He'd have to get rid of the kids that night, they'd ruin it, show him up, make him look old, keep calling him 'Dad'.

'Oh, that would be lovely. When?' (Was she sounding too keen?)

'Um, Wednesday?' (That gave him nearly a week.)

'Oh, we can't, the café . . . but we are closed on Sunday nights . . .'

'Sunday then?' he asked.

'Great. I'll just tell Paul. He won't be doing anything unless it's a bird-watching thing or something.'

Every room in John Vir's house was painted blue, sky blue, a shade that in a smaller expanse might have been nice. The floors were covered in lino in a pattern of orange bricks. There were no books. The sofa seemed cast from concrete. The younger Virs had put up some Formula One posters, and there were pictures of Ganesha the elephant god and Shiva, and a puppies calendar dating from Mrs Vir's time. Those puppies would be at least great-great-great-great-grandparents by now. It made Lucy want to cry, 'But all it needs is a woman's touch!' like Doris Day's friend in *Calamity Jane*, and to quickly run up some pretty gingham curtains. They had brought a bunch of pinks for Shreela.

'So, Shreela,' said Lucy, 'do you run a shop as well?'

'I'm a barrister.'

'Oh, right . . .' said Paul.

'Shall we eat?' said Shreela, and she strode away on neat navy blue legs.

The table was set for four. The young Virs had seemingly been banished or had deserted. It looked like a real dinner party, white household candles from downstairs burned. His plan was taking shape.

They had poppadoms, of course, with hot lime and brinjal pickle, Paul's favourite. They were going to pig out. Shreela told them about her practice. She had often seen Cherie Booth at dinners, but they hadn't actually met.

John Vir was busy in the kitchen. He wrenched open cupboards, fumbled crazily amongst half-empty packets, crumpled paper napkins, greasy jars, petrified sugar, spices that had turned to dust. Not there! Not there! He slammed doors shut and skidded down the orange lino stairs to the shop. Boxes tried to trip him, bales of loo paper jostled him, a supermop bopped him on the head.

Yes! there were a few packets there, behind the Lucky chicken noodles: MSG flavour enhancer as used in all the best restaurants and take-aways in Southampton. 'Use Very Sparingly' the packet told him.

113

'Dad, how much are Kotex Superplus?' yelled Gurpal from the front of the shop.

'£1.73,' he called over his shoulder, as he sped towards the stairs.

'Do you want a little bag?' Gurpal asked the student girl who for some reason looked close to tears.

'It hardly seems worth it now,' the girl said, as Gurpal tried to cram the packet into what was a very little bag. 'I'd better have some paracetamol too.'

'What are you *doing* out there?' Shreela called.

'Giving it the finishing touch,' John Vir called back, smiling at his unintended pun.

'You want some help?'

'NO!'

Two white unbreakable plates with orange borders were carried in.

'Ladies first,' he said, and placed them in front of Shreela and Lucy. A deep yellow curry on a fragrant pile of multicoloured rice. He brought in the dhal, the plate of warm chappatis, another dish of aubergine, one of okra. 'All vegetarian tonight,' he said. Paul's plate had a dark green border, his own an orange one. They tucked in.

'This is great,' said Paul. 'Just like from a take-away . . . that's a compliment. I mean, it's great.' He drained the water jug into his now smeary glass.

'Too hot for you?' asked John Vir, a little spitefully.

'No, I'm just really thirsty,' said Paul.

'Paul is one of those thirsty people, you know, always having a glass of water,' said Lucy, but they didn't seem to know. 'This is really delicious,' she went on, racking her brain for something to say.

'Oh, Shreela did all the hard work,' said John.

'I love to cook,' said Shreela. Now they should be on safe territory.

'Oh, so do I!' said Lucy, even though a vision of potato peelings in cold, muddy water, of damp, gritty yellowing spinach leaves, of the last time she had grated her thumbnail on the cheese grater loomed behind her eyes. 'Well, sometimes I love to cook, it's different now that I do it for a living, and a not very good living . . .' Paul looked a bit surprised and hurt at this.

'Could I possibly have some more water?' he said.

A red fist was biffing the back of his skull. His heart raced. He was sweaty and freezing and boiling. He lurched into the bathroom and made it just in time. He managed to run his face under the cold tap, gulped mouthfuls, gallons of water. It was 2 a.m. He wished for death.

At 7.15 Lucy and Fennel discovered Paul on the bathroom floor, lying under a towel. His head was resting peacefully on the scales and weighed one and a half stone. Fennel licked his salty face and headbutted him. Lucy knelt down and put her hand on his cheek.

'I think you'd be more comfortable in bed,' she said.

All he could say was: 'Gnu.'

She went to the all-night garage, Vir's being out of the question, and bought milk of magnesia, Tums in five fruit flavours, some Alka-Seltzer and a packet of Clorets for them to share.

'There,' she said, tipping her haul on to the bed. 'Which would you like first?'

'Alka-Seltzer,' said Paul, 'and tea?'

'It can't be anything you ate,' Lucy told him, a note of impatience in her voice. 'I'm perfectly all right.'

'I'm not being ill on purpose,' he told her hostile back as she stomped away to make the tea. She brought him the tea in his favourite yellow mug, not considering how like the colour of cauliflower curry it was, and a piece of dry toast. Her own fat wedge was smeary with butter and Marmite.

'I do feel a bit funny too,' said Lucy. 'Perhaps we shouldn't open today, we might poison the customers.' She knew it was the thin end of the wedge, the first step on the slope of only opening when she felt like it, but she didn't care.

John Vir heard sirens in the night. They called to him through the darkness, luring him to the window. He leaned out and craned his neck to see where they were. There were lights on at the Bluebird Café, but no ambulance arrived. 'Damn,' he said, and cracked the back of his head on the window frame. A fox was tearing open the bin bags and strewing garbage across the pavement outside the shop. Its coat glowed double orange, under the street lights. Leftover catfood and stale samosas made for sleek, fit foxes. John Vir wondered whether it preferred the meat ones or the veggie ones. Meat probably; they were spicier.

Paul's attack of food poisoning lasted for two days. It left him paler and thinner.

'My belt's on the third notch,' he told Lucy for the fifth time. Lucy wished she'd had it. She thought that she ought to lose half a stone. She'd been thinking that since she was nineteen.

Paul refused to go into Vir and Vir for a week, too

embarrassed to say thank you for the meal that he thought had nearly killed him. Lucy went round with a bunch of anemones for Shreela, but she was too late. Shreela had gone back to London.

'Oh, you keep them,' she told John Vir. 'I can't take them away again.'

'Get a vase or something, Gurpal.' He jabbed at his daughter with the flowers. Gurpal came back a few minutes later with an empty Holst curry powder tin and plonked the arrangement on the shelf behind the till, in front of the Rizlas and the Red Band. Lucy knew that a bunch of desiccated stalks would mock her for ever.

John Vir knew that something must have happened to Paul. Nobody could eat that much MSG and not be ill. For a while he hoped that Paul might have died and Lucy not have realised or bothered to do anything about it. Then he spotted Paul cycling past. It seemed that he'd have to think of something else. He started to make a list on the bottom of his Cash and Carry one.

1. Run him over with the van.
2. Different poisoning.
3. Push him off a train or a cliff.
4. Fight in a pub.
5. Bribe him to leave.

It occurred to him that perhaps he didn't have to get rid of Paul; perhaps he could come between them, lure her away, get her out of that café and into his arms. Gurpal plonked herself down on the counter.

'Fat chance,' he said.

'What?'

'Nothing.'

'Dad, can I have 50p?'

'No.'

'Why not?'

'Just no.'

'What'd'ya bother having me for if you won't even give me 50p?'

Perhaps she'd like to go and visit her mother. Without noticing what he was doing he punched the Cash button. Gurpal's hand shot forward to grab a few coins.

27

S ummer was good for business. Despite Gilbert's continual presence the Bluebird was flourishing. The tables were sometimes full, and they were making a bit more of a profit. They bought another freezer and began to sell ice creams through the window. Lucy found the supplier with the prettiest of flavours and chocolate-lined cornets, New Forest Ice Cream. They wished that the pavements were wider so that they could put some tables outside. Teague kept pointing out that they were selling ice creams on one of the oldest roads in Wessex. It had been a Roman road, and a Saxon one too. Lucy needed more help. Paul was being elusive, in demand at the Badger Centre, covering for the centre manager who had now moved to East Anglia, having been off sick for a month with a suspected slipped disc, probably caused by trying to move the beehive all by herself. Abigail was at a crucial stage, so she said, with her research. Lucy made a notice on some cardboard, cut in the shape of a fat pigeonish bluebird. PART-TIME GENERAL ASSISTANT AND ICE-CREAM SALESPERSON REQUIRED. APPLY WITHIN.

But the first applicant was already inside and had watched the notice go up.

'Is that a new notice, Paul?'

'Er, yes, Gilbert.'

'For some more artists to bring their pictures in for you to put up?'

He read the ad to Gilbert. He had noticed that Gilbert was a bit hazy around words.

'Paul,' said Gilbert, 'I can certainly help you out some more. I'd like to work for you some more. Would I be good enough for the job?'

'Well, I'll have to ask Lucy. I'm not sure what she's looking for, the hours might be wrong for you, it is her café, she's the boss of it . . .' He put the notice up in the window and strolled nonchalantly into the kitchen, where out of sight, he knelt on the floor and banged his head again and again against the chiller. Lucy came in carrying an ice-cream scoop.

'Mr Heathcliff, I presume,' she said, then knelt beside him and cradled his head in her arms so that he had to stop. Paul looked up at her. She was flooded with love. He reminded her of Fennel.

'What's wrong?' She hardly ever asked him that.

'Gilbert wants the job.'

'No way,' said Lucy. 'Just no way. Absolutely not.'

They told Gilbert that he'd have to wait – it was only fair – someone unemployed might need the job, someone with children or animals to support. Gilbert said that he'd wait and see. He made sure that he wiped the tables extra thoroughly. He brought Lucy his collection of Shippam's Fish Paste jars (with labels) for extra vases. He brought *What to Look for in Autumn* and *Keeping Finches* for Paul to read. Paul put them in a carrier bag under the counter. The question of employment for Gilbert was put on ice. They were waiting for more applicants. But no more applicants came.

'What we are looking for,' said Lucy, 'is someone very good-looking, dark, tall, possibly Mediterranean.'

'What you are looking for,' said Abigail,' is someone capable, with clean fingernails, who won't cough at the customers.'

Gilbert had a very persistent cold and a rather chesty cough. Lucy gave him a sticky bottle of Benylin that Mr Snooke had left behind. It didn't seem to work. The job poster was taken down and not mentioned, and then Paul finally got around to looking at *What to Look for in Autumn* and saw the inscription: 'To Gilbert, on your 10th Birthday, from Mr Dove.'

There could only be one Mr Dove. Paul asked Gilbert about it and found out that they'd been at the same school. About ten years separated them, but they were both alumni of Penshurst Village School (C of E Maintained).

28

M r Dove built the weather station himself to his own design. It looked like a bird table. There was a maximum–minimum thermometer, a barometer, a funnel and a beaker for catching and measuring rainfall, and a weathervane. He hung up long tails of seaweed and pine cones too. The weather had been monitored every day (in term time) since his first week at the school in 1960. A rack of grey and buff exercise books held records of the prevailing conditions in a corner of the school field outside the science-block window. Mr Dove hadn't missed a single day of his teaching career through sickness. He had been asked several times if he was a Christian Scientist. He wasn't. He just never seemed to suffer from colds or upset stomachs the way his colleagues did. He was the only male teacher at Penshurst School, and he sometimes wondered if women were more sickly than men, or took time off work more lightly, but he would never have been ungallant or provocative enough to voice these thoughts. Instead, he was punctual and reliable. He poured oil on the troubled waters of many staff meetings. He championed underdogs. He organised the teams for cricket, rugby, football and rounders, and pinned his selections on the green baize noticeboard beside his class-room door. Every morning he swapped his soft green tweed jacket for one of the crisp white lab coats that his wife laundered so nicely. There was always a spare one waiting in his carefully locked science cupboard along with the pencils and exercise books, the rulers and rubberbands, the lime water and copper sulphate solution, the magnets and iron filings, the batteries (which he called cells) and the circuit boards, and the test-tubes, beakers, pipettes, funnels and other pretty glass instruments with their carved wooden racks and metal clamps.

Mr Dove never showed favouritism, but there were some children whom he thought about very often and whom he would remember. Paul Cloud was one of them. Paul Cloud, aged nine, had noticed the pawprints of a fox in the mud beside the weather station and had spent his lunch hour making a plaster cast of them. Paul Cloud found the body of a female wood-boring wasp and brought it in to show him. He had never seen one before. It had taken them all of morning play to identify it. Paul Cloud was a very reliable weather monitor.

Ten years earlier Gilbert was shown how to be a weather monitor. Mr Dove helped him to read the thermometers and measure the rainfall (although the beaker had been practically empty). They'd written down the wind direction (W) together and looked at the clouds (cumulus). A few weeks later Gilbert went to take the day's readings all by himself. Seven inches of rain. The temperature had ranged from −2 to +28. The wind was blowing from the south. Gilbert wrote it all down and put the 'Weather Journal' in the special tray on Mr Dove's desk, hoping for some words of praise, a Well Done in front of the whole class.

'What is this, Gilbert?' For once, Mr Dove could hardly conceal his irritation. 'Come here!'

Gilbert dragged his sad feet towards Mr Dove's desk. What had he done now . . .?

'Your weather report,' said Mr Dove. 'These figures cannot be accurate.'

'But, sir . . .'

'Did it rain last night, Gilbert?'

'I don't know.'

'Minus two, Gilbert. Has it been cold enough for ice to form? And twenty-eight degrees. Was it the hottest day of the year? What was the weather like yesterday and last night?'

'I don't know. Was it just plain weather?'

'Plain! What is plain weather? It was cloudy and mild. It was not hot or freezing. I am almost certain that it didn't rain. Now, Gilbert, tell me the truth. Did you bother to check the weather station or did you just make these readings up?'

'I did check it, sir. I tried my best to.'

'Well, Gilbert,' said Mr Dove kindly. 'Either you need more practice as a weather monitor, or somebody unkind has been playing a trick on you.' Mr. Dove scanned the classroom. Thirty-two heads were bent over their books. Two pairs of shoulders were shaking. Sheila Pye and Theresa Welch. A spiteful pair.

'Sheila and Theresa, what are you finding so funny?'

'Nothing, sir,' they spluttered. How could old beaky Dove know that they'd been there after netball practice with an ice cube, matches, a cup of water and Sellotape for the weather-vane?

Gilbert would never forget those words, would now always doubt what his senses told him.

'Either you need more practice as a weather monitor, or somebody unkind has been playing a trick on you.'

29

G ilbert's teeth were a chipped, yellow monument to a life alone, a life without love. A Stonehenge To Neglect. He had a huge, scruffy, pinkish toothbrush with splayed bristles. It had given years of faithful service. It hadn't occurred to Gilbert that he had no dental records to be used in the event of the Wayside burning down or his body being fished out of the Itchen. His last brush with the dental health services had been twenty-nine years ago: a stern school dentist had urged more frequent brushing, and given him a free toothbrush, some paste and a number of fillings. Vestiges of these remained. Sometimes a bit of filling or tooth would break off and cause him some pain for a while, but it generally went away.

Gilbert had never known his father, but he took after his mother, Lily Runnic, as far as teeth went. Her brittle teeth had led indirectly to her early death. She'd been on her way home from the chemist with the week's supply of oil of cloves when she collided with a milk float, banged her head on the kerb, and never regained consciousness. The air at the scene of the accident had hung heavy with the scent of cloves for days afterwards, she'd been getting through three or four bottles a week. It turned the milkman's stomach at that corner every day until he had taken early retirement. The dairy had sent a wreath of milky-white chrysanthemums to the funeral. It had been the only one, no lilies for Lily. Gilbert hadn't known about floral tributes and things like that, and nobody told him how things were normally done.

In Mr Dove's classroom, the science room, there were posters of molecules in liquids, solids and gases. Gilbert read it as 'mole cures', medicine for moles. They did experiments with felt pens and filters (paper chromatography it was called), and lime water and carbon dioxide. This was before there was a hole in the ozone layer. Science and Nature were Gilbert's favourite lessons.

Gilbert always arrived at least an hour before school started. His mum gave him two slabs of bread and paste, breakfast and lunch. He sat on top of a concrete tunnel in the corner of the playground to eat the first one, neatly round and round the edges, to leave a perfect pink disc. The other children played, ignoring him. Gilbert had warts on his knees and prickly fingers with chewed nails and grimy plasters. Mr Dove saw this sad leprechaun each morning when he and his wife arrived at the school, rolling towards the staff car park in their green Morris Traveller with its window stickers from Canada and the Bluebell Railway, Mousehole Seagull Sanctuary and Gweek Seal Rescue Centre.

This morning the children sat cross-legged on the floor of the hall which was also the dinner room and the gym. They could hear the canteen ladies behind the hatch. Tinned tomatoes, soft watery quiche and boiled potatoes, and semolina with blobs of strawberry jam. The teachers sat on a neat row of chairs at the back, Mrs Dove (PE and Maths) grimly knitting. Mrs Ford, the headmistress, was standing on the stage saying that everybody must be kind to Gilbert because his mother had been killed in an accident.

Mr Dove's chair, on the end of the row, was empty. He was walking round and round the football pitch with Gilbert who was aware that he, the last to be picked for any team, had finally been chosen for something. There was a fairy ring beside the goalposts. Gilbert pointed it out to Mr Dove who said, 'Yes, yes.'

When Mr Dove said: 'I expect you'll have some time off school,' Gilbert said: 'But I'm meant to be a weather monitor again next week!'

The boy didn't seem to be grasping what had befallen him. Mr Dove felt a depression descend. When their next circuit passed the fairy ring, Gilbert kicked over all the tiny toadstools to make it rain.

'They have an underground network, Gilbert,' Mr Dove couldn't resist telling him. 'Hyphae of mycelium.'

Mrs Dove had never especially liked Gilbert; but then he wasn't a particularly likeable child. She sat through the special assembly, knitting. She dropped three stitches in annoyance when she saw her husband walking back towards the hall and Gilbert carrying a balled-up handkerchief, an initialled one that the twins had given Ian, and she herself had ironed. How typical of the boy not to have his own with him. She retrieved the stitches and jabbed the needles into the ball of wool, even though a friend of hers had insisted that it could lead to pilling and bobbling later on in the life of the garment. She marched off to make herself a cup of tea. Her navy T-bar shoes clicked across the staffroom floor.

And yes, it turned out that she was quite right to be annoyed. Ian came back with some nonsensical scheme about fostering and then adopting Gilbert. She soon put a stop to that. They'd had their children, a set of twins, who were in their second year at Cambridge, reading Medieval History and Biochemistry.

So it turned out that nobody came to Gilbert's rescue, nobody took him in, nobody helped. Nobody ever does.

Gilbert's Auntie Vi arrived to organise the funeral, but she had to get back and she wasn't taking Gilbert with her. He was sent to 'The Elms'. For the next eight years he rarely wore an outfit twice.

The clothes were kept in tea chests. It was first come, first served, and by the time Gilbert fought his way to the front there was only ever a bizarre jumble of things left. He once had to wear a girl's blouse. He rolled up the flouncy yellow sleeves to disguise it. Luckily it wasn't a PE day.

There was a big TV in the sitting room. When it rained they all watched *Blue Peter* and *Scooby Doo* and *Vision On*. Gilbert wished that he had a grown-up to help him make some of the things they showed. Collecting boxes and paper and things was really hard. He wished that he had some paints and some glue.

The Elms had a garden, though. There were some huge sighing trees where wood pigeons lived, and a shed with a window and a bench where Gilbert could sit. Sometimes he saw squirrels.

30

Maggie Cloud (capable hands, neat polished nails) shredded orange tissue paper into pretty ribbons for Paul and his sister, Kate, to use to pack their harvest boxes. Mr Dove organised the collection, and after a special assembly the children took the baskets of goodies to local old folks.

'Mum, Mr Dove wouldn't mind brown paper,' Paul told her.

'What's this?' Kate asked.

'Asparagus. It'll be a special treat for someone.'

There were two pots of Maggie's home-made raspberry jam, two jars of her green-tomato chutney, two warm fruit cakes, decorated with concentric rings of almonds, two oranges, six apples, four bananas, two tins of Baxters Scotch Broth, two very small marrows and two jars of peaches preserved in brandy, all for the pair of them to pack.

'Isn't it a bit good, Mum?' Kate asked, as she did every year. She knew that her friends would bring damp cardboard boxes with cans of S&B baked beans and Smedley potatoes and butter beans, tins of custard powder and packets of Bourbons. For some clever children, Harvest Festival was an occasion for ridding the store cupboard of hated groceries. Tins of carrots, tins of prunes, whole cabbages and packets of blancmange found their way into the boxes. Mr Dove once retrieved a half-empty bottle of banana-flavoured antibiotic medicine from a harvest box. It was sent home with a note.

At the beginning of the Harvest Festival the children

marched across the stage and plonked their boxes on the trestle tables that Mr Dove and Mrs Field (Music) had covered with greengrocers' grass. This grass would endure for ever. It could withstand a nuclear strike. It was just as sharp, bristly and shiny as when ten years earlier Gilbert had brought his own harvest basket. It was a soap-powder box, one side cut off, almost all of the washing powder gone. Inside were some bendy leeks, a packet of biscuits and some windfalls. His mum had helped him. Her nail scissors had made deep pink ditches on his pudgy fingers as he'd tried to cut through the heavy card. In the end he'd sawed out a panel with the breadknife.

But the next year his mum was dead and he had nothing to bring. The kitchen ladies at The Elms said that there was nothing spare, even if it was for Harvest and God. He was summoned to see Mr Dove. He didn't want to tell him that he had nothing to bring, but he'd have to.

'Ah, Gilbert. Come in.' Mr Dove's plain, calm face appeared around the door of the science cupboard. 'Could you help me with these please, Gilbert?'

And there on the bench between the gas taps and the sink was a cardboard box and a green canvas holdall of provisions.

'There's paper here for you to decorate the box; scissors, glue, coloured pencils. Make sure you put them back in the right trays. You should have plenty of time.'

There was half of dinner play left. Gilbert wouldn't be missed on the football field or by the groups playing trumps or jacks or French skipping.

'You can leave the box here tonight where it'll be safe. Collect it before assembly tomorrow.' Mr Dove pushed his stool under the bench where it couldn't constitute a tripping hazard.

'Yes, sir. Thank you, sir.'

'It's the very least I could do, Gilbert.'

And Mr Dove wanted to hold that small, breakable boy. To stroke his unbrushed, unwashed curls, to make things all right. But he didn't.

'And, Gilbert,' he said, 'if there's any way that I can help you, please come and find me.'

31

The Badger Centre Management Committee met on the second Wednesday of the month. Their meetings were watched by the newts, rats, ants, wood mice and assorted fresh-water fish and creatures of the Solent Estuary, the Centre's permanent residents. Paul always felt that they should be listed in the minutes as 'in attendance' along with the other non-voting members of the committee. The minutes were printed on a special type of recycled paper, unique to the Centre and guaranteed to jam any copier or fax machine. It had been made by a workers' co-operative of local wasps. The committee was chaired by Cllr Bette Doon (Lab). The first time Paul had seen her, he thought that she was a female impersonator. She seized every opportunity to squeeze people's arms and give hefty, jocular pats on the back. Paul always tried not to sit or stand anywhere near her.

There was only one item on the agenda that really interested Paul: 'This Month's Sightings'. He didn't give a damn about 'Staffing Issues' or 'Fund-raising' or 'Treasurer's Report'.

'A pair of goldfinches have been seen eight times feeding in the heathland area. Cuckoos have been heard on numerous occasions. Fifteen pairs of tufted ducks are nesting beside the cemetery lake. This month there are twelve known cygnets, the highest number since records began six years ago.' Paul fell into a reverie. The meeting continued. Some minutes later he heard himself agreeing to take part in a sponsored whittling event for the Badger Centre and the New Forest Owl Sanctuary.

'What a hoot!' quipped Cllr Doon.

Hoots of derision from Lucy, Paul thought. He wondered who he could ask to sponsor him. He decided that he'd just have to invent the sponsors and donate all of the money himself.

Outside in the Centre grounds a hedgehog trundled across a tiny bridge, briars twisted above a path, making a bower for a silver tabby cat who was waiting for mice, or perhaps to take part in the Official Government Bird-Ringing Project. That afternoon Lucy and Paul had sat on one of the many 'In Memory' benches, and Lucy had silently vowed that henceforth she would wear only the colours of the hedgerow.

Old man's beard, old man's beard, thought Paul to himself, But what is its real name?

Someone was lurking in the bushes, waiting, waiting for the meeting to end. A rustling of greaseproof paper and the reflective strips on the arms of her anorak betrayed her. She was wishing that she'd brought along a flask of Horlicks, there was nothing really warming about her piccalilli-and-paste sandwich. The damp was seeping through her plimsolls and socks, and underneath her skirt, her calves were blue and mottled.

Cllr Doon always seemed surprised to see her, even at the Councillors' Surgery where Mavis dropped in each Saturday now, with something new to report on her windows, her housing benefit, the terrible state of Kingsland Market, there was always something to talk about.

Cllr Doon had noticed that some of the newer councillors didn't hold surgeries, they just said that they would visit people in their own homes, and who would want that? She was thinking of dropping her surgeries, or at least her St Mary's one which Mavis now thought of as her own. She had once scolded Mavis quite harshly for trying to bar the way to a group of young mums who wanted to see her about the closure of the After-School Club. Mavis was saying that the double buggies would block the exit and be a fire risk, but Cllr Doon knew that Mavis just wanted the time all to herself. She'd barked, 'Be quiet, Mavis! Stand back. Let the little children come to me!' Mavis had sulked outside eating Wagon Wheels.

Wagon Wheels were Mavis's favourite even though the soft mallowy discs gummed up her mouth whether or not it was encumbered by teeth. Her passion for Wagon Wheels had brought to an abrupt end one of her attempts to do a bit for charity, to get out more. She was asked to leave the League of Friends when she was caught cramming half a dozen of them into her bag. There had been other reasons why they'd wanted her to leave, her habit of cleaning her fingernails with knives that were meant for buttering scones, and the time she was suspected of filching three copies of *Woman's Weekly* from a partially-sighted patient who had, sadly, passed away.

Here she was now, waiting for Cllr Doon. She wanted to talk to her about something, and if Cllr Doon had her car then Mavis would make sure that she got a lift home. After all, she didn't want to be wandering around on the Common in the dark, did she?

When the Badger Centre minutes arrived in their mouse-scented brown envelope ten days later, Paul discovered that not only had he volunteered to take part in the sponsored whittling event, but that it was to take place in the Bluebird. The date was familiar. Oh yes. Lucy's birthday.

32

Minutes of the Meeting of the Badger Centre General Committee
11 May 1999 at the Badger Centre. 7.30 p.m.

Present: K. Watts, D. Mellish, P. Tupper, J. Tupper, K.
Tupper, C. Polls, P. Cloud, Cllr Doon (Chair), A. Wallis.

Apologies: J. Fielder, K. Stoops.

Matters arising from minutes of 10.4.99.
1. The wind-damaged bird table has been replaced. Thank you,
   Paul.
2. The water vole has been seen four more times.
3. The fire extinguishers have now been checked and serviced.
4. The date of the first-aid course has been changed from
   10.8.99 to 11.8.99. All staff, volunteers and committee members are requested to attend.

1. New pond
   The new pond will be dug on 20.5 from 9 a.m. P. Cloud, K.
   Tupper and J. Tupper all volunteered. Others welcome. A
   newt-moving licence has been granted.

2. Fundraising
   The sponsored whittle is going ahead, but will now be on
   June 26. (NB A post-meeting change of date by arrangement
   with the Bluebird.) Thanks to the Bluebird Café for offering
   refreshments, etc. Our next event will be a stall at the Balloon

and Flower Festival, first weekend in July. Stall theme to be decided at next meeting. Volunteers required to staff it. D. Mellish to draw up a rota.

3. Leather Bookmarks
   At the request of two vegan members, leather bookmarks will no longer be sold at the centre. Current stock (approx. 12 bookmarks, assorted colours) will be given free to the next school party.

4. Treasurer's Report
   In the absence of the Treasurer there was no Treasurer's Report. The Treasurer will be asked to submit a written report when she is unable to attend meetings, especially as this often seems to be the case.

5. Staffing
   The Centre Manager's position will be advertised in the *News* next week. Interview panel will be P. Tupper, Cllr Doon and C. Polls. Agreed to ask the successful candidate to start ASAP, to ensure the bird-ringing project is properly supported. Contract renewable annually. Salary £17,695, or less if the Woodman's Cottage offer is accepted.

6. Sale of Animals
   Several requests have been received to purchase mice and rats. It was agreed that these would ALWAYS be refused, even when funds are low and the animals are breeding well. Visitors will be encouraged to buy toy mice instead. The possibility of introducing an adopt-an-animal or sponsored-mouse scheme will be discussed at the next meeting.

7. Any Other Business
   The Chair thanked K. Watts for delivering the newsletters despite the rain.

8. Date of Next Meeting
   16.6.99. Would all committee members please ensure that they arrive PROMPTLY.

'What's this about the Woodman's Cottage?' Lucy asked. Her reading of the Badger Centre minutes was more usually punctuated by snorts and cries of 'Ha!' than questions.

'The Centre Manager can live in that little cottage on the edge of the Common if he wants.'

'Or she. Is it nice?'

'A little bit damp, untouched inside since the fifties. Surrounded by bluebells and wild garlic and a ditch full of celandine, and cow-parsley hedges. It's really called "Bluebell Cottage"'

'Oh, Paul, apply!'

'I didn't think you could manage the café on your own.'

'I hate the café. We'll sell up. I'll find something else to do.'

'I had kind of thought about it.'

'I'll make marzipan animals and felt mice for you to sell at the centre!'

Paul saw himself sitting in a deckchair in the Woodman's garden, listening to the cricket.

'The money's good,' he said.

'Better than we make here.'

'And we'd get rich quick with the marzipan animals . . . but I am on the committee, isn't that sort of unethical?'

'But you practically do the job already. I'm sure they'd snap you up. You're the best they've got, the only person who isn't over eighty or completely doolally, a total twitcher. Go on. Ring up for the form. Do it now, then you can just leave a message on the machine . . . Would you need a new suit for the interview?'

'I hadn't thought . . . It wouldn't matter really. They know what I'm like.'

'Perhaps you should just wear a lumberjack shirt and carry an axe?'

Paul wore his old suit. Lucy had found it in Romsey Oxfam. She made special trips to Romsey, Lyndhurst and Lymington where the second-hand shops were full of rich people's cast-offs. Paul had a tweed jacket with a moss-coloured lining. Lucy had found a yellow cashmere scarf with a silk lining (and only one tiny burn mark) and a proper panama hat that rolled up, and a pith helmet which they hung on the wall, thinking that it would be of questionable taste to wear it in the inner city. Lucy's favourite skirt was a black circular one with ribbons round the bottom. She'd found it in Lymington Help the Aged. She had a genuine Burberry from the same shop, but it had bust darts and they made her feel silly.

There had been thirty-seven enquiries about the job and the Badger Centre's Recruitment Subcommittee were pleased with their drafting of the ad. It had taken three meetings and five phone calls to the *News*. But only nine application forms were returned. One was completely illegible, and one contained no information except the applicant's name and address. There was one which said: 'I love all animals, especially badgers. My friends tell me that I am a kind of a person and good with working with the children and the animals, although I am not very keen on insects like moths.' These were put on the Definitely No pile. There were four recent graduates with little relevant experience, and an unemployed youth worker. Paul's application shone like a glow-worm.

'We'd better interview him though,' said Pat Tupper, sipping her Blackcurrant Bracer fruit tea.

'Equal Opportunities – yes!' said Cllr Doon. 'Thank The Lord he applied.'

'Shall we have a couple of the Biology ones to make the numbers up?' Colin Polls suggested.

'Good idea, Colin. And, Pat, could you write to all the no-hopers please, say intense competition and if they'd like to volunteer . . . all the usual stuff.'

Pat made a note in her notebook. 'Shall we plan the questions now? We can ask about their hobbies.'

33

'Aldi is the cheapest,' Mavis said, spitting egg sandwich. 'And these aren't sausage rolls,' she continued, jabbing one at Gilbert and then Cllr Doon. 'Not real sausage rolls.'

'Of course they're real,' said Gilbert. 'Feel one.'

'No, I mean, there's no meat in them. Euch!' And she stubbed it out into a parlour palm pot.

The sponsored whittling event was about to begin. Paul and Lucy had over-catered. There were ten participants, most of whom were just sponsoring each other. The photographer from the *News* hadn't arrived yet. They were all given sticks which Ken Tupper, one of the Badger Centre volunteers, had gathered on the Common that morning. Paul's seemed to be a bit damp. A woodlouse walked out of it. He took it to the back garden and tapped it gently against the step, making a family of the mini-armadillos homeless.

'Uh-oh,' he said out loud, and put the stick under a bush, 'sorry, chaps.' He found another piece of wood and took it back inside.

'I'm telling you, Aldi is the cheapest. No arguing.' Nobody was arguing with Mavis, least of all Cllr Doon, who was planning what she would say to the deaconess she was meeting once she'd got away from the whittle. The deaconess wanted a grant of £37,000 for repairs to a church hall. Bette Doon just didn't know if a grant that big could be justified, even if the hall was used by the Silver Oldies Lunch Club and three troupes of baton twirlers. She had agreed to meet the deaconess that afternoon and join her on the city's 'All Faith March for Peace and Reconciliation'. It was to end with prayers at the cenotaph.

'They do household as well,' Mavis went on. 'There's something in the *Advertiser* every week, the special offers. This week it's blinds for £7.99. Peach or plum. I'm going down there now. I want a peach one. And rotary dryers. £8.99 including the cover. So no arguing! It's even cheaper than Lidls without the bus fare. Coming then?' She thrust her chin at Cllr Doon.

'Sorry, my dear. I'm already booked for the "All Faith March". In fact, I must set off now, mustn't be late, goodbye!' Bette tried to make a speedy exit, she dropped the stick that she'd made a poor attempt at whittling into the umbrella stand on her way out, but her sleeve caught on the door handle and she was trapped.

'Wait for us,' Mavis called after her. 'Come on, Gilb, you'll get some bargains. And my trolley's lost a wheel so you can give me a hand.'

'So you're off your trolley, are you?' Cllr Doon quipped.

'What?' Gilbert was confused.

'They'd like you to go with them,' Lucy explained, 'to the shop or on a march in the town, near the cenotaph.'

'Cenotaph? What's that?' he asked.

'That big white blocky memorial thing near where the Aviary used to be.'

'Oh,' said Gilbert. That made sense to him. He stuffed some cheese straws and apple shortbread into his pockets, and shuffled after them.

'I didn't know he knew them,' Lucy said when they'd gone.

'Maybe through the council or something. It's not through the Centre,' said Paul.

'Maybe she works at the council. Perhaps she's a cleaner.'

'I thought she looked like a dinner lady. She might be in the canteen,' Paul suggested.

'Did you see her nails? She really couldn't work in a kitchen. Talons!' Lucy told him, 'Huge black and yellow claws. Imagine her toenails. Rhino's feet. Ugh!'

Lucy pictured Mavis's toenails hanging over the end of some thick rainbow flip-flops.

'What?' Paul asked.

'Oh, I think they might be quite well suited, Gilbert and that woman,' she said.

'Hmm.' Paul wasn't listening now, he was concentrating on his whittling. His stick had a particularly tricky knot that looked a bit like an owl.

'Is this it?' Cllr Doon asked the deaconess. She hadn't intended to sound so scathing.

'We were hoping for a few more, but the Methodists have cancelled, an inter-church badminton match. A pretty poor excuse really. We're hoping for some more Sikhs but there's a big wedding on at one of the Gurdwaras; either that or a Death in the Community, I expect. The Baptists have just gone to get their banners. We'll be setting off soon. Did you bring any instruments?'

'Just my voice,' said Cllr Doon with a smile. She was heavily tipped to be the First Mayor of the Millennium.

34

Mavis's lounge was a shag-piled shrine to Kenny Rogers. Her pride and joy hung on the wall above the settee. It was a huge towel, bought at Southsea Funfair; a portrait of Kenny with his guitar standing on a mountain top surrounded by crotchets and clouds and quavers. She had almost all of his records as well as mugs, T-shirts, pictures, a clock with his face, and a mirror where, unless she jumped or ducked, it was Kenny's face that stared back at her. The effect was uncanny as they had hair of the same colour and style.

'I'm not one of these Johnny-Come-Lately-Lucille Kenny fans. I've always loved Kenny,' she explained in her head to imaginary people who might ask her about her collections, and to the few visitors that she managed to lure into her parlour for tea and a slice of lardy cake. She bought a slab of yesterday's every day at the baker's, which was one of the last businesses still running in the sad parade of shops that bordered the estate. The butcher's was long gone, the post office was packing its bags, and market forces had forced the 50p Shop to change itself into a 55p Shop.

'Sit down here, by the fire, love,' she told Gilbert. 'Get yourself warm before you help me with that Venetian and that dryer.'

The gas fired at the fourth attempt. Orange and blue tongues licked at the decaying honeycomb and danced outwards into the room. She brought in the huge red BOVRIL mugs and two chunks of cake. The tea was steaming strong and milky, and she heaped sugar into Gilbert's mug without asking if he took it.

'Lots of children in your family?' Gilbert asked, indicating the cardboard boxes full of jumpers, mittens, cardies and hats, and the carrier bags that were spewing balls of wool, needles and patterns on to the floor.

'Only some nephews and nieces in Shirley that I don't see much,' Mavis said. 'I knit for the cats.'

'Uh?'

'Sick cats, rescued cats, strays . . .'

Gilbert supposed that the mittens must be for bandaged paws and the other stuff for when they lost fur or had the cat flu which he knew was a killer. But wouldn't knitwear be a bit dangerous for a cat who was climbing trees, or going through hedges or whatever?

'Would be good for those small dogs that shiver too,' he suggested, thinking of chihuahuas and Mexican hairless. 'Knitting for some dogs would take just as long as making something for a grown-up. Great Danes and Alsatians and them are just as tall on their hind legs.'

'What? Why would I want to knit dog clothes? I might knit you something one day,' she said, with a lusty glint in her eye. 'What are your measurements then?'

'Um, medium, I think.'

The Southampton Cats Protection League gave a collective miaow of horror each time Mavis arrived to donate one of her boxes of knitted items. She never missed a fund-raiser. At the Autumn Bazaar, Christmas Fayre, Spring Bring and Buy and even the Summer Beach Bar-B-Que, there was always a stall heaving with her handiwork. She knitted with a special kind of itchy acrylic wool in shades that nobody would ever choose, and in styles that hadn't been worn for over twenty years; balaclavas with peaks, matinée jackets with huge buttons, scratchy pram-suits, jumpers with arms long enough for a gibbon. The secretary of the League took them with her when she visited her mother in York and made anonymous donations of them to a PDSA shop there.

'Come here,' Mavis told Gilbert. 'I'll get your measurements.'

He splashed his mug down on to a Kenny coaster and stumbled towards her with his mouth and arms open wide.

When he awoke the next morning, the pink-and-grey marbled slab that was Mavis's arm was pinning him to the bed, and the grey-and-pink ham that was her calf was lying across his legs. Kenny's face told him 6.30. Time to make tracks for the depot. He tried to slither out. Mavis woke.

'You can't go to work on an empty stomach!' she told him and she was soon resplendent in a pale blue towelling dressing gown, the cuffs stained brown by tea and fry-ups, doing him some eggs.

Gilbert wasn't the sort to worry about wearing the same underwear twice, but Mavis lent him some, and it fitted.

'My late husband's,' she told him. 'And my first late husband's before him.' Gilbert felt honoured.

'I don't always do this, you know,' Mavis told him.

'Oh, I don't need cooked breakfast every day.'

'Not the eggs!' She clouted him playfully and painfully with an old copy of the *News*. 'I mean sleep with someone on a first date!'

'Nor do I,' he told her, 'but you're special.'

151

'You're Special'. A slogan that he'd seen on sashes worn by white rabbits and teddies holding red hearts in a card shop window. He'd wondered what they were for, and now he knew. He thought that he might get one for Mavis if they weren't too expensive.

Staying for breakfast at Mavis's meant that Gilbert missed breakfast at the canteen. He'd have had eggs, tomatoes, beans, sausages, bacon and toast there. He thought about this as he trudged to work and decided that it was well worth it.

35

John Vir decided that undercooked kidney beans might be the thing to try next. He'd stuff a samosa with some and give it to Paul when he came into the shop on his own. Who could resist just one samosa? It wouldn't get anywhere near Lucy. If that failed he'd ask Paul to help him with some decorating and push him off a very tall ladder. The way to Lucy's heart would be clear. Gurpal's project had told him that kidney beans should be cooked thoroughly, boiled for four hours, something like that.

He soaked a handful of beans overnight and then cooked them for fifteen minutes, just to soften them up. He stirred them into some samosa-filling mixture, and wrapped it up making a square to distinguish it from the rest of the batch. He carefully lowered it into the boiling oil, it fizzled and turned orangey-brown.

'Giz one, Dad!' Gurpal's quick hand reached for the biggest one, the square one.

'No!' He slapped her hand away.

'Aw, Dad, why'd you bother to have me if you won't even give me a samosa?'

'OK. Have one. Just one.' He handed her a neat triangle.

'Why'd you bother making them when we've got half a trayful left downstairs?'

'We can't always be eating the stock.'

He carried a plateful of them downstairs and sat behind the

counter, watching the cricket with the sound turned down and the radio commentary on, waiting for Paul.

Paul was in the café listening to the cricket while Lucy made pies and four customers spent an hour over three cups of coffee and a glass of tap water, and two chocolate shortbread biscuits. He could sense that they wouldn't leave a tip. Lucy ran out of eggs. He waited for tea before he nipped out to Vir's to buy four boxes of their eggs which claimed to be free range and were certainly mucky. On the box there was a picture of a hen standing under an apple tree.

'Probably kept in a shed with one tiny window,' he told Gurpal who was putting cartons of Happy Shopper orange juice on shelves. She didn't reply. He picked up a coconut to cut in half for the birds and headed for the till. John Vir told himself to Act Natural. As Paul approached he bit into one of the home-made samosas.

'Nice to have something to eat when you're watching the cricket.'

'Lucy makes me lemonade,' said Paul. 'Good for when it's really hot.'

'We used to make ginger beer. I'll find the recipe for you. Here, try one of these.' He wrapped the square one in some kitchen roll and gave it to Paul. 'Ketchup? I got a bottle here.'

Gurpal kept a bottle of ketchup under the counter to anoint stolen samosas and pakoras. He brought it out. The neck was clogged red and black, as though decapitated in a terrible accident.

'I'll pass on the ketchup, thanks.' He bit into the samosa and John Vir gave him a strange look when he handed over a fiver.

'No, no. On the house.'

'For the eggs,' Paul explained, 'and the coconut.'

'Oh, those eggs. £4.56.'

John Vir piled them into a blue-and-white stripy polythene bag so thin that Paul hoped that sunlight might break it down before it was landfilled.

'They're coming out again,' he nodded towards the screen.

'Light looks bad though,' said Paul.

'Might not last long.'

Paul left. He hurried to make it back to the café before play resumed. He dropped the samosa into a bin around the corner. He'd kind of gone off curried things since that meal at the Virs'. Back at the café he saw that the four customers had left him a 10p tip. A Jersey 10p.

'Cheers,' he said, and put it in the box that they kept by the till.

John Vir spent the afternoon watching the cricket. It seemed like a good omen when India finished the day on 186 for 2.

Lucy came into the shop at ten to ten for paracetamol.

'Paul isn't well?' he asked her.

'No, they're just for me. Headache. That's all.' She was feeling sick too, kind of dizzy. 'Too long slaving over a hot stove,' she told him.

'You need a rest.'

'Mmm. I know. One day.'

Lucy's 'one day' was to live at Howards End, or somewhere pretty similar. Perhaps with a walnut tree and an orchard.

'I'd like to keep bees,' she told him.

'What?'

'Oh, one day, we might move to the countryside, retire or do something else, you know . . .'

She could see herself reading in a hammock in the orchard, sitting in a beechwood steamer chair in the sun, coming back from the orchard with a basket of apples, or walking through the garden with a trug full of flowers or raspberries. Fennel was there, twining around her legs or sprawled on the hot flagstones. Paul was there too, somewhere, and there might be children playing in the apple trees.

Later that night, John Vir heard music coming from the café which was closed. At first he thought it was Lucy singing and Paul playing the violin, but then the whole orchestra joined in and he could make out some of the words. It was something about cigarettes, strangers and ashtrays.

He looked out of the window and saw Paul, not in his death throes, but walking along with that funny lope he had, carrying a rucksack. Outside the café he patted his pockets, dumped the rucksack on the pavement and started to search in that. No keys.

Then Lucy opened the door. The light shone bright behind her and she was as flat and thin as a Fuzzy-Felt figure, a ballerina from Gurpal's Fuzzy-Felt set, so long ago. The bright yellow board, like the light streaming out from the café now, the figures suspended. There was no floor, just flat sky, there were white felt birds (Gurpal called them seagulls, he told her that they were doves) and flowers and ballerinas and one male figure who could wear a blue cloak.

He saw Paul look up, surprised at the open door, and that

Lucy didn't step back to let him pass, but opened her arms and tilted her face upwards for a kiss. There was no stumbling, they were a pair, perfectly choreographed.

'Dancing to their own music,' John Vir told himself. And he knew that he shouldn't interfere, that they should be happy together. He remembered how upset Gurpal had been when a Fuzzy-Felt picture had been scrambled back into the box. 'I will love her from a distance,' he told himself.

The next day, John Vir was cutting up fresh chickens at the back of the shop. He had a sharp, strong cleaver worthy of an appearance on *Crimewatch*, that thwacked through flesh, separating wings and limbs from bodies, bone from flesh, spirit from soul. He rarely cut himself. The last time had been just after Mrs Vir left. He'd almost sliced off his thumb. He had worn a huge clumsy bandage for days. The loss of sensation made him feel giddy and underwater, even now as he thought about it. He decided to think of something else. Mmm, Lucy. Then he remembered his resolution. He would take them a present to make amends. Paul seemed to have survived that samosa. He looked around the shop for a present. Paper plates, ones that nobody would ever buy, thin and bent. No. It would look like rubbish. Plastic cups. No. A saucepan. They must have all that they needed. It should be something proper, not just excess stock. He could cook something, but perhaps Paul wouldn't trust his cooking again. Then he thought of ginger beer plants and the recipe he'd offered Paul. Perfect. He'd copy it out and take it round that afternoon, or maybe later that week. He could get Gurpal to type it up for him at college. It would be good practice for her too. Thwack. He finished the last of the chickens. He'd done forty of them that morning, a special order for a wedding. He tipped the bucket of entrails, necks and feet on to some newspaper, parcelled it up and put it into the huge metal trade waste dustbin where the foxes might not get at it.

36

' A w, Dad,' said Gurpal. 'What for?'
         'The café people.'
'But why?'
'Being neighbourly, Gurpal. They can use it in the café.'
'What'll you give me?'
'Quid.'
'OK.' She shoved the recipe in her bag.
'I want it today, my girl.'
'Money upfront.'
'Cash on delivery.'
'Aw, Dad.'
'Come here.'

Gurpal slouched towards him. He kissed the wonky parting on the top of her head and gave her a pound from his pocket.

'Dad.' She pushed him away, but he thought that she looked a bit pleased.

Gurpal gazed through the Computer Studies window into the greyness outside. There were some pigeons pecking around a drain, but nothing or nobody worthy of her attention. She was meant to be doing spreadsheets, but she'd missed the last few lessons and wasn't quite sure what they were. She found the recipe her dad wanted typing and hoped that it would look like a spreadsheet.

Her lips moved slowly as she read:

GINGER BEER

1. Grow a Ginger Beer Plant with 2 oz baker's yeast in a jar with $\frac{1}{2}$ pint water, 2 level tsp sugar and 2 level tsp ground ginger.

2. Feed it every day for the next seven to ten days by adding 1 tsp sugar and 1 tsp ground ginger. You will see your plant getting bigger every day.

3. Strain the mixture through a piece of muslin or a very fine sieve. Keep the sediment. It will make two new ginger beer plants, one for you and one for a friend. To the liquid add the juice of 2 lemons, 1 lb granulated sugar and 1 pint boiling water. Stir until the sugar has dissolved, then make up to 1 gallon with cold water.

4. Bottle the ginger beer. It must be kept for seven to ten days before drinking. Leave three inches breathing space in the top of each bottle and leave for two hours before putting the caps on loosely. Do not stand the bottles on a stone floor.

'Gurpal Vir! What is that?'

Mrs Merstham's clicky red nail stabbed at the screen. Gurpal tried to melt, to slide lower into her chair.

'Is that a spreadsheet?' Mrs Merstham demanded.

'I dunno, Miss.'

'What is it then, Gurpal?'

'Um, nothing, Miss . . . just a recipe. My dad wanted it typed.'

'Well! Do I deliver this module to enable students to type favours for their families?'

'No, Miss.'

'Then get rid of it.'

'Yes, Miss.'

'I want that spreadsheet finished and on my desk by the end of the period.'

'Yes, Miss.'

There was a cry of despair from the other side of the room. 'Carrie Chitty, what is wrong now?'

'Saved!' Gurpal told herself as Mrs Merstham hovered over her next victim. Gurpal clicked on Save and then Print. She had most of the recipe done, all the ingredients and that.

'What the fuck's a spreadsheet?' she asked the girl sitting next to her. 'Giz yours.' She set to work copying it. The numbers wouldn't stay in their columns, but if you read it diagonally it was more or less the same.

37

'Here you are, Dad.'

John Vir was surprised. Gurpal never gave him anything. It was the ginger beer recipe.

'Did it at college for you, didn' I.'

'Thanks, love. Here you go.'

He gave her two pound coins from the till, forgetting that he'd already paid her, and that they'd agreed on a pound.

'Thanks, Dad.' Gurpal was out the door before he might realise his mistake. It was neatly typed. He smiled. Gurpal was good at this anyway. He folded it into one of the brown paper bags he usually used for samosas and put it behind the till. He'd take it round later that evening.

Lucy was alone behind the counter with a book when he walked in. There were just two occupied tables, students eating puddings. Lucy was surprised when the door opened. Not many people came in after nine. She looked up, annoyed. She didn't want to do any more dinners. She hoped that they'd just want coffee. Then it was him.

She shoved her book under the counter – a girl caught reading in class – she bit her lip, gave a guilty smile. John Vir was coming towards her with a very flat paper bag. She blushed, felt silly for blushing, blushed even more.

John Vir just saw Lucy, pink and pretty, smiling at him.

'I've brought you something, for your café. Instructions.'

'Instructions?' Lucy thought. 'What, business tips? Getting customers? Increasing profits?' She drew the folded sheet out of the bag, feeling like a celebrity announcing an Oscar.

'Gurpal typed it at her college,' he told her.

'Well, it's really neat, tell her. Give her my congratulations,' she said. It sounded silly, but she couldn't concentrate to read what it was. She tried harder, focused.

'Oh, a recipe. Thank you! Ginger beer. I've always meant to do this. We'll definitely have a go at this. Thank you! It's really kind.' And before she thought of what she was doing she came out from behind the counter and kissed him on the cheek.

The black clouds lifted.

The sun shone.

The ice in his heart melted.

The frog turned into a prince.

The Disney bluebirds sang in the corners of his mind,

And

Snow White threw open the shutters to a beautiful new morning.

38

'I 'm not sure how long Abigail will be here for,' said Lucy.
'I didn't know she was here. She doesn't usually do
Thursdays, does she?' said Paul, his eyes drifting back to the
tray of Shasta daisies that he was pricking out.

'Can we eat those?' Lucy asked him.

'They aren't nasturtiums. Or marigolds.'

'But can we?'

'No.'

'She's applied for a place on a dig in Suffolk. Teague
too.'

'Him . . .'

'It's a two-year project. They'd move. They'd have to live in
tents at first. Abigail says she wouldn't mind, but it'll be a
different matter when the perfect bob is iced over.'

'Ha!' said Paul, who wouldn't really miss them very much.

'And Teague's feet would suffer. He'd probably insist on
wearing his high-performance sports sandals in the snow . . . I
don't know how Abigail can be in love with someone who
thinks that those are acceptable footwear. Or who has such a
self-indulgent name, or who is so keen on medieval things.'

'But, Lucy, some of the medieval gardens must have been
very beautiful.'

'Imagine a world without potatoes and tomatoes. Just turnips,
and lice in your armpits. And you'd be old at thirty. I know. I
did it for A level. Even Robin Hood probably didn't exist. It

would be really hard to manage without Abigail. I don't want anyone else involved!' she railed.

'I could help out more . . .' Paul started to say.

'You don't want to though, do you?'

'Well . . .' He obviously didn't.

'I know what'll happen. I just know,' said Lucy. 'Gilbert will find out and try to "help" and even bring his girlfriend. We've got to be firm with him. Oh, Paul, can't you just tell him to get lost, make him go away?'

'None of this has happened yet. He was at my school,' Paul said, anything to avoid unpleasantness.

'But not at the same time as you! Ten years before you!'

'He is an orphan too.'

'He's nearly forty! He'll ruin my café.'

'Be kind, Lucy,' said Paul, and she felt like Emma Woodhouse shamed by Mr Knightley: 'It was badly done, indeed.' But it wasn't fair. She was quiet for a few minutes.

'I can't stand it much longer, though. The smell of damp, Old Holborn and bins. I know he loses us customers.'

'We weren't exactly turning them away before Gilbert arrived,' Paul said, trying to be fair.

'Can't you just hint that we don't want him here every afternoon?' she pleaded.

'Can't you? Anyway, he doesn't come every afternoon any more, not since he found Mavis,' Paul pointed out.

'Is that her name? Doesn't suit her, does it? It sounds too thin.'

'She hasn't really got bright eyes and a lovely voice,' said Paul.

'Bet she's got a spotty chest though.'

'Ugh.'

But Lucy knew that Paul wouldn't say anything to Gilbert. Somehow, without appearing stubborn or selfish, he managed to avoid doing anything he didn't want to do. Lucy didn't know that he'd honed this skill as a boy, slipping out of the conversation and out of the room whenever Maggie Cloud's enthusiasms for French conversation or clearing out the garage or whatever became too much. He might just wander away, or he would back out of the room smiling, shaking his head, hands raised in mock surrender, keeping any threat to his tranquillity at bay.

Abigail and Teague heard about the dig a week before Abigail plucked up the courage to tell Lucy. She decided to leave it until Lucy would have guessed anyway, hoping that Lucy's first wave of anger or sadness would have passed before they spoke. She bought Lucy a present to say sorry, a print of shells in a bluey-green frame, it might as well be a leaving present. The dig started in a few weeks. She didn't want to fall out with Lucy, but this dig was too good an opportunity to miss.

Lucy wasn't surprised when Abigail told her. She pretended to be pleased for them and said, 'Don't worry. I'll find someone else to help me. Maybe a nice sixth-former. If they're really young I won't feel so guilty about paying them a pittance.'

'But they might eat all the cakes. Teenagers are always starving. You'll have to dock her wages if she eats too much. Maybe you should get an anorexic.'

'Might put people off.'

'Well, don't get a bulimic! Think of the waste!'

'I'll make it an interview question. "What kind of eating disorder do you have?" And if they say "None", I'll say, "Oh, you must be in denial." Well, as long as they aren't really skeletal or obese, it's clean fingernails, nice breath and no spots that really count.'

That night after they locked up and Abigail and Teague (who had been drinking Newquay Brown and laughing out loud at *A Prayer for Owen Meany* which Abigail had given him for Christmas two years ago, but which he had only just got around to reading) had left, Lucy told Paul.

'They are going on that dig.'

'I thought they would. When?'

'Three weeks.'

'You've got plenty of time to get someone to help you then,' said Paul, forgetting that he'd offered to be that someone, but everything was different, now that he'd been offered the Centre Manager's job.

'I don't really want anyone except Abigail.'

'But you might need someone.' She saw the shadow of Fear Of Being Dragged In cross his face.

'I might get a sixth-former. Or just try to manage on my own for a bit. I'll just have to get up earlier. I feel like throwing the towel in,' she said, chucking some dirty tea towels towards the washing machine. Paul smiled. 'No, really, I do. It won't be much fun without Abigail.' Her eyes were full of tears. 'I'm too tired.'

'I will help you, Lucy.'

'I have been thinking about quitting. Except I don't know what else I could do. A PGCE maybe.'

'I didn't know you wanted to be a teacher.'

'I don't.'

'Then don't.'

What Lucy really wanted that night was someone with £20,000 a year and very many acres in Derbyshire; but she thought that she couldn't tell Paul that.

'I'm going to bed,' she said.

'I'll make some tea,' said Paul.

'Camomile, please.'

Lucy drank the camomile tea. It usually made her sleepy. Paul was already asleep and looking at home in the world. Lucy thought about her life. Somehow she had expected exciting things to happen. She didn't know what she wanted to do now, let alone for the rest of her life. Abigail and Teague would always be happy digging. Paul would just consider the lilies of the field and the birds of the air and be content. She thought about her ex-friend Sara whose name she saw every Saturday in the *Independent*. Sara would definitely be happy. Lucy hadn't kept in touch with all of her friends from school or university, but she knew what most of them were doing, and it was impressive. They were all doing something; travelling, being doctors, working in TV, making lots of money. Not running a café for losers. She bet that Sara's hands didn't smell of tinned tomatoes or onions. Lucy sniffed her hands again. It made her feel sick. An odd sickness like a lump at the top of her stomach. She sat up and that made her feel even sicker.

39

'Aren't you going to ask then?' said Mavis, flicking her ash into the crinkly paper case of the last Fondant Fancy.
'Ask what?' asked Gilbert.

'What happened to the others!'

'I just saw you eat them, didn't I?'

'Not the Fancies, you daft bugger. My husbands!' Mavis shouted, playfully punching him in the arm. 'Everybody asks sooner or later.'

'You don't have to tell me, Mavis.' Gilbert said kindly. 'I don't mind about your past.' Gilbert hadn't really thought about Mavis's past, but now that he did, he thought that he didn't really want to know.

'I'll tell you,' she said. 'I met me first husband, that was Les, when I was just ten. He was from a big family that moved into our street. Everyone knew the Diapers.'

'Oh,' said Gilbert, confused by the name.

'Les Diaper knocked me up when I was sixteen. My mum talked to his mum. They settled it all and we was going to get married. But I wasn't, after all, and then seeing as I had the dress and everything we got married anyway. He worked on the ships. He was killed cleaning inside of that tanker. The *Endeavour*. That was the biggest one ever in Southampton.'

'I remember it, that ship,' said Gilbert. It had taken up the whole horizon. It was so big that people hardly believed it could move, but eventually it did, sliding out of Southampton Water

171

to in-depth coverage on *South Today* and a double-page spread in the *News*.

'He was cleaning it. They had to go inside where there wasn't light and scrub with these chemicals. He fell eighty-five feet.'

'What happened?'

'Well, he died, didn't he, stupid.' Mavis was annoyed now. 'They said it was his own fault cos he was eating a Marathon. They weren't meant to eat on the job. Even tried to say he choked to death. Eighty-five feet and they said that!' Gilbert patted her shoulder to try and calm her down. Her face was getting redder and she was scratching her arms harder and harder making a rasping sound, long thick nails across skin that was hairy, leathery and shiny.

'I met my next husband – that was Wilf – at the funeral. Wilf had been on the same platform with Les when it happened. He saw everything and he said that you couldn't see much as it was black in there.' She paused to light another cigarette. It calmed her. 'I'll show you some photos sometime.'

'You've got photos?' asked Gilbert, incredulous. 'Of that?'

'What?'

'Of him dead in the ship?'

'Whaddya think I am? Who'd have photos of that . . . Would you want to see'm? You a pervert?'

'No!' cried Gilbert, helpless. 'I didn't understand, I thought you meant . . .' His voice trailed off again. Perhaps he'd blown it with Mavis now. He didn't want to see photos of her dead husband, or even husbands.

'Oh, come here, you,' said Mavis, all forgiving. 'You're just daft.'

Gilbert's eyes were brim-full as he buried his head in the soft pillows of her chest.

Three days passed before Gilbert thought to ask: 'But what happened to Wilf then?'

'Heart,' said Mavis. 'Out of the blue. He looked fit as a fiddle but he just dropped down dead in the bookie's.'

'I'm very sorry to hear that, Mavis,' said Gilbert, and he took her hand.

'So was I. He told me he'd given it up. I didn't believe them when they phoned me up. "It's a Case of Mistaken Identity," I told them, but they came round and got me to identify him. I was livid. He had dockets for £25 in his pocket and the manager said that there might be others I could get back, but I'd of had to fill out the forms, and seeing as I didn't know what he'd put on, I couldn't, could I?'

Mavis blew a fat smoke ring. It drifted towards Gilbert, the ghost of a wreath.

'And they're bloody miles from each other!'

'Pardon?' said Gilbert.

'Wilf and Les. In the Garden of Remembrance. It takes me fifteen minutes to get from Les to Wilf, and sometimes I forget to say something and I have to go back, then back again. You can come with me next time I go, if the weather cheers up.'

'OK,' said Gilbert, but he wasn't sure if he really wanted to go.

'Don't look like that!' Mavis gave him a hearty nudge. 'We can make a day of it with sandwiches and a picnic.'

The number 13 bus trailed through the Flower Estate. There weren't that many flowers, but wrecked cars, Union Jacks, rotary dryers and whole *Argos* catalogues of toys had sprouted in the gardens. In Begonia Road the soil was heavy clay. There were a few brave-hearted begonias and busy Lizzies. Autumn would bring garden mums. Every few yards the bus stopped so that huge girls with strong bare legs and pushchairs could clomp on. Pensioners heaved themselves aboard. Dusty felt hats, scarves, macs, trolleys, cracked purses with bus-pass pockets; they had everything necessary for a trip to the shops in the kind summer sunshine.

'All right, love?'

'Not so bad. Yourself?'

The bus drivers called them Twirlies because their passes became valid at 9.30 in the morning and they were always asking: 'Am I too early?' A driver had been disciplined, and disgraced in the *News*, for setting his watch ten minutes slow.

The bus lurched around a sharp bend and plummeted downhill past Daisy Dip where there were grass and swings and trees and things to ride.

'That's where they want to build the new houses,' an ancient in a purple tea cosy told her headscarfed companion.

'No!'

'It is. Housing association. You know what that means.'

Her friend didn't, but nodded sagely.

'Pakis and more kids.'

'They can't do that to Daisy Dip!' But they could, and would.

Gilbert fingered the change in his pocket and looked at Mavis holding the picnic bag, clamping the handles together lest any goodies should tumble out or get nicked. It was only 9.55. Gilbert wondered how long they'd wait for the sandwiches. He guessed that they'd visit the graves first. He hoped that Mavis wouldn't get upset. He'd hate it if she cried.

Mavis had brought a bottle of Kleenezee Spic'n'Span, all-purpose Polish'n'Kleen and some Happy Shopper J-cloths for the headstones and the flowers. Gilbert had a pack of cards in his pocket. He was looking out of the window, he hadn't been this far north in Southampton for a long time. The houses got further apart, they were off the Flower Estate now, just a few miles from the village where he'd grown up.

'Come on!' Mavis shoved him and his shoulder banged against the window. It would have hurt but for the thick padding of Wilf's tartan jacket with its big furry collar. The zip was broken but it still had plenty of wear left in it. Silly not to accept it. So Wilf's jacket was visiting Wilf's grave. Gilbert hoped that Wilf wouldn't mind. He had felt a bit awkward wearing it there, but Mavis had said that his council coat was disrespectful.

They swung down the aisle and off the bus. As it pulled away Gilbert realised that he'd left his return ticket tucked into the metal trim of the seat in front of theirs. Oh well, too late. He dreaded telling Mavis.

Mavis didn't cry. She worked hard with the Spic'n'Span, and the graves and flowers were soon sparkling.

'Wilf, this is Gilbert Runnic,' she said. 'Say hello then, Gilbert.' She gave him a subtle kick in the ankle to prompt him.

'Hello, Wilf,' he mumbled.

'He's with me now, Wilf. We might get married. I know you won't mind.'

'Us? Get married?' Gilbert's mouth fell open.

'Why not? We love each other, don't we?' She hurled herself

towards him, intending to fall into his arms, and for a moment they stumbled, and Gilbert thought that they were going to collapse on to Wilf's plot.

'We'll do it properly, mind. I'm gonna ask Cllr Doon to be my back-up.'

'Back-up? What for? If you don't show up?' Gilbert hadn't even said 'Yes' yet, and he was in danger of ending up with Cllr Doon if Mavis dipped out at the last minute. She might too. He had no idea what this crazy woman might do next.

'Witnesser, I mean. To sign with us.'

'Oh. I haven't ever been to a wedding yet . . . Could I ask Paul and Lucy?'

'Everyone loves a wedding. Come on, let's celebrate. Where's that thermos?' She grabbed the bag and unzipped its side pocket, it grinned back at her with white plastic teeth. 'Here. I brought these to sit on.' Out came two neatly folded plastic carriers. Gilbert's said 'I'm A Happy Shopper', Mavis just had a Lloyd's Chemist one. They unpacked the picnic and got comfy, leaning against the mossy old stone behind them, where six feet under was Lily Runnic (1925–1965), resting in peace.

40

S mells. Lucy was surrounded by them, overcome by them. She hadn't realised before what a smelly place South- ampton was. Ugh. The smell of the fake-fur collar on the tartan jacket that Gilbert had taken to wearing. Grease-clogged nylon. A man came into the café and Lucy knew that he'd had a boiled egg with Marmite soldiers and a drink of milk for breakfast. The smell of a customer's dirty hair. The smell of dirty tea towels. The smell of the mice and the Badger Centre. She could tell that Paul had cleared out the newts that afternoon.

'Paul. The smell of newts, or even worse, tadpoles, is the worst smell in the world,' she told him, but he was making himself a peanut-butter-and-cheese sandwich and she had to leave the room before he could reply. She pulled the neck of her sweatshirt up over her nose and breathed through that. She wished that Abigail was there to do the frying. She bought some cologne tissues at the chemist so that she could carry one balled- up in her hand and sniff it when necessary. If this carried on, she decided, they'd definitely have to quit the Bluebird, or serve nothing but very, very weak peppermint tea, melon, and lavender sorbet.

It must be a cook's ennui, Lucy decided. A special nausea that a person would get if they'd cooked too many hot dinners. Then she noticed that her feet had a new splayed look, as though something had been dropped on them, or a cartoon steamroller had rolled over them. They were flatter and looser.

Paul, even Paul, noticed that she looked tired. She had huge panda circles around her eyes. Her wrists ached. Her lips were chapped. The words were in her mouth.

'Paul. I think I might be pregnant.' She didn't say them because she couldn't believe it might be true, and didn't know what she would feel, but she had a sneaking suspicion that she might be VERY PLEASED. She decided to do a test and then tell Paul if it was Yes, and perhaps if it was No.

The Boots Home Pregnancy Test Kit, £7.95, was in her bag – bulging, she joked to herself, a surely unmistakable bulge – when they looked around Bluebell Cottage.

'Lots of plants are original,' Paul told her. 'Nineteen twenties. The bulbs have naturalised. I saw it last spring, all blues and yellows, scilla, real daffodils, and bluebells of course.' The gardens were surrounded by a thick hawthorn hedge and a ditch. There were front and back gates with little bridges.

'Ha ha – a ditch!' said Lucy. 'I'd have to make that joke to myself every time I went out. I wonder if it will flood.'

'No, silly. Too high up,' said Paul.

'Oh. I never really think of Southampton as having hills.'

'There would have been deer here once,' Paul said. 'There's a badger sett not far off too. We could go and watch at night.'

'What's this?' asked Lucy. It was an unusual tree. 'Is it native?'

'It's a wychelm.'

'Oh, Paul! Really?'

She looked for pig's teeth. There weren't any, but even better, there was a walnut tree with a swing.

'We could put a hammock up too,' said Paul, 'and get some more deckchairs.'

'I'll make pickled walnuts. We'll be self-sufficient in them. Let's go inside.' There was a black iron boot scraper and a bell pull.

'Mr Badger, I presume,' said Lucy.

'What?'

There was a porch with shelves for geraniums and a place for wellingtons and spiders. The door was heavy. There was a brass knocker, a woodpecker. A pokerwork sign said 'Bluebell Cottage'.

'Do you think that's naff?' she asked Paul.

'Sort of, I don't know. You'll have to ask Abigail,' Paul replied.

'Well, I hardly think that someone in love with someone who wears sports sandals can be the arbiter of good taste.'

'I suppose not.' Paul unlocked the door with a very ordinary Yale key. Inside everything seemed pale yellow. It made Lucy think of retsina, or a yellowish Chardonnay. All of the woodwork was painted yellow. The floors were all bare boards and had once been polished; they would be again.

'There is gas,' said Paul, 'but it has to be serviced, and probably all replaced, but that's a landlord's legal duty. It comes unfurnished. Apart from this—' he tapped a hatstand '– and there's a table in the kitchen.'

'Could we have real fires?'

'Once the chimneys have been swept. Wouldn't you mind living on the Common? You couldn't go anywhere on your own after dusk.'

'Where is there to go? I never go anywhere anyway. And it's only a few yards from a road.'

'Cemetery Road.'

'Well, that's a gay pick-up place so I'd be all right. We could always move again if it was too spooky or something . . .'

'What about your café?' Paul asked her. 'You know I can still do the job without taking over the cottage. They'd be paying me more too.'

'Oh, let's forget the café, ditch the café. There's only two more months to go on the lease anyway. Now's a good time to quit. Quit while you're breaking even, isn't that what they say? And something might happen. I might do more for the *News* or get another job or something. The café's no fun now that Abi's gone.'

'You'll miss her, won't you?'

'I haven't got anyone to be friends with now.'

Lucy didn't know that there was a whole new raft of friends waiting for her a few months away. Friends to go to Aquanatal with, to float beside, their arms entwined in buoyant, bendy, pastel-coloured poles, friends who would keep each other afloat, who would pass around bootleg copies of a recently published study on Squash-Drinking Syndrome in Under-Fives, friends to meet by the duck pond, all carrying un-necessarily huge changing bags and endless supplies of bread-sticks and baby wipes, friends who would tell each other they were looking really slim (or really tired, cream-crackered, saying 'Have you had an awful night?'). Friends who all carried spotless white muslin squares from John Lewis. Lucy would want to send Paul out to buy some. She hadn't known how indispensable they were.

Pretty dust motes danced in shafts of sunlight that were sliding through the sitting-room windows.

'I used to think that they were bits of gravity,' said Lucy, 'and that the sun's rays were ladders for angels. It's really warm. I was expecting it to be cold, and you said damp.'

The kitchen seemed cold though.

'We can paint it, and once we've got the oven on . . . and it might be sunny in here in the mornings.'

There was a proper larder with marble shelves and a pointed wooden door. The cracked grey lino ran out a foot short of the back of the larder, revealing dusty red tiles.

'Quarry tiles! We can be on *Home Front!*'

Upstairs was a bathroom with a huge enamel bath full of spider webs, and a sink with coppery trails under the taps. The loo had a hateful brown plastic seat.

'We'll change the seat and bleach everything. It'll be fine,' said Lucy.

'There isn't a shower.'

'I don't mind.'

There were two bedrooms, one was really tiny.

'There wouldn't be much space for people to come and stay,' said Lucy.

'Good.'

The smell of emptiness and some dead flies on the windowsill made Lucy feel sick again. She opened the window and breathed in great draughts of the sweet woody air. They could see a section of one of the paths that circled the lake. Birds were singing. A pair of dog walkers strolled past, swinging their leads, dogs nowhere, then came a boy on a bike, then a jogger.

'I think it's quite busy here actually,' said Lucy.

41

Paul and Lucy locked up Bluebell Cottage and set off back across the Common towards the café.

'I do love it, Paul. I mean, I would love to live there. I'm sick of the mean streets of Southampton. It's so dirty around the café. I know every crack in those dirty sidewalks . . . Really, we should think of moving right out into the Forest, or the real countryside.' Lucy had never been quite convinced by the New Forest's claims to be an Area of Outstanding Natural Beauty. It was too accessible and reminded her of childhood walks across some of Surrey's finest golf courses. You always seemed to be within a *Hawkshead* catalogue's throw of a Renault Espace. 'Would you like that, Paul?' she asked. He looked surprised.

'Yes.'

They were almost at the Badger Centre now.

'I just need to check some new sea anemones . . .'

'Paul! Oh, OK. I'll wait outside.' The smell would be too much. Lucy sat on a bench beside a bright green frog litter bin. She patted its warm plastic head and considered kissing it. Paul came out carrying a very small fishing net.

'They need clearing out again. I'd better stay. Do you mind? You can come in.'

'Oh, I'll just go home. I've got things to do.' She could do the test on her own and think about the results, and telling Paul.

A blue line appeared on the little white tile. Lucy smiled at herself in the mirror. What to do now? The luxury of quiet contemplation, the excitement of having a real secret.

She made a salad of nasturtium flowers and watercress and took some of her best rolls out of the freezer, plus a brazil roulade. Thank God the café was closed. Then she had a bath and washed her hair and put on the dress she'd bought for Vicks' wedding. She checked the café lease. Two months left to go or a month's notice to give. They could sell the café stuff – tables, stove, chillers – and buy a pram or a cot or something. Perhaps the Badger Centre would buy some of the stuff. She'd ask Paul. And she could maybe start doing teas there, just really nice cakes and biscuits on Saturday and Sunday afternoons. Mmm. She could make little biscuit animals and teasels and bees and things. She couldn't stop smiling.

Paul came in two and a half hours later. Could cleaning out the sea anemones really take that long? She didn't ask. He'd probably done the crayfish and the fish and the ants as well. He noticed her dress.

'Are we going out?'

'Not unless you want to.'

'Looks nice.'

'Thanks.' She'd intended to tell him over dinner. She couldn't wait and she still couldn't stop smiling, but how to pick the words, the best line of her life?

'Paul, I think I am, I mean, I am, um . . . pregnant. I mean, having a baby.'

'What? What?' He stepped backwards, shocked or backing away . . . 'That's brilliant!' His long, thin, aquarium-smelling arms were around her. He was kissing her hair, breathing in its dark marigold sweetness.

'Are you pleased?' she asked.

'Yes. But when, how long have you known? I didn't really notice anything.'

'Nine months, I suppose.' She counted on her fingers. 'September, October, November, December, January, February, March, April, May, June! I don't know exactly when you start from.'

'It's forty weeks, I think, Lucy, from the first day of your last period.' He could picture the table from A-level Biology, and how the human one had compared to a cat, rabbit and horses. Lucy was slightly taken aback when he said 'period'. He didn't usually discuss hers.

'Sit down, rest!' he said, propelling her towards the sofa.

'I do feel sick all the time, and everything smells.'

'I'll make you a cup of tea and some dinner.'

'Really weak. I've made the dinner already.'

Paul went to make the tea, but kept looking at her all the time and smiling.

'It's so lucky that we're both pleased,' she said.

'Marry me, Lucy.'

'Can we get some things sorted out first? I mean, sorry, yes, I will.'

They kissed.

'I don't want to renew the lease on the café. Let's just go and live in Bluebell Cottage. If we sell some of the café stuff, I think we can end up even. And I've got some ideas for the Badger Centre. I want to do teas.'

'You might have enough to do just with the baby. I think you should go to the doctor's tomorrow and get it all checked,' he said.

*   *   *

185

Lucy went to the doctor's. She was weighed (64.8 kilos), and was given a Pregnancy Pack, a blue vinyl folder with charts and notes and leaflets. Once the lunches were finished she bunked off from the Bluebird and walked into the city centre. She got her hair cut and bought some folic acid tablets and *Pregnancy and Birth* magazine. She drifted round Mothercare, looking at impossibly small clothes, and bought a catalogue. Everyone else seemed to be pushing pushchairs, the occupants of which were either cross or asleep, or chewing something, or swigging something lukewarm from a bottle. Hmm. But then Lucy's baby would never eat in its buggy, or cry in shops, or have a red face, or wear a stupid headband or anything with a slogan on.

42

I t was the Bluebird's last week. They were moving out on Sunday.

'I don't know if Gilbert and Mavis are having a honeymoon,' Lucy said. 'A coach holiday might suit them. A *News* Readers' Club special excursion. Or one of those Couples Only Pay Upfront and Eat All You Want islands.'

'What about us?' Paul asked her. 'We could have a honeymoon if it wasn't too expensive.'

'Not a couples resort. There'd be salad bars.' Lucy had a horror of self-service salad bars. So unhygienic. And dips. People who might double-dip. Ugh.

'Impossible,' said Paul.

They looked in the back of the Sunday papers and decided on the Isles of Scilly where Lucy had always wanted to go, and where Paul had been as a child, and the Clouds had dined in some of the South-West's Finest Fish Restaurants. Lucy didn't want to go really abroad because of the baby. They would get married in early October at the registry office, just like Mavis and Gilbert, then have some friends back for a Wedding Reception/Gathering/House-Warming sort of thing at Bluebell Cottage. Lucy kept wondering if she wanted a white wedding, a church service, cars, all that stuff; but she decided that she didn't, which was lucky, as they couldn't afford it, and didn't want to ask their parents to pay for anything.

Paul was to wear his good Romsey Oxfam suit with a yellow

silk tie and new shoes, not even £14.99 desert boots, but actually 'Chukka boots' that cost £39.99, whatever Chukka boots were.

'Hope it doesn't mean "Chuck 'er!"' said Lucy, who had bought a caramel velvet dress with an ambiguous high waist from Monsoon, and an almost matching hat with dark brown velvet roses on. She thought of an autumnal bouquet: teasels, brambles, rowan-berries, bryony. They could have had the reception at Paul's centre. They'd be attended by squirrels, young badgers, bumble-bees and robins who would throw autumn leaf confetti. She drafted a guest list and showed it to Paul.

Abigail and Teague
Parents
Relatives
Other friends from university
All staff and volunteers from the Badger Centre
Soo Sholing from the *News*

Did they really have to invite Mavis and Gilbert? Should they invite the Virs? They would be ordering four dozen samosas from them.

'Do you think we have to ask Gilbert and Mavis? We might have managed to shrug them off by then?' she asked.

'Didn't I tell you? Gilbert's a regular volunteer at the Centre,' Paul said.

'No.' Angry silence. 'What about the Virs?' Thank God Paul had never noticed any of that stuff, the frisson, the electricity she thought that there'd been between her and John Vir. Thank God she'd never let it go anywhere. It all seemed silly and distant now. 'We could ask Shreela and John and Gurpal, but not those boys.'

'Do you think they'd really want to come?' Paul asked.

'I don't know. They are our friends, sort of.'

'I don't think we have to bother,' said Paul. She crossed them off.

43

1973 Graham Buildings
Kalimpong
India

Dear Jagdish,

Am writing to come back to England. Please send £400 or dollars for ticket. Gurpal phoning so I will be back when money arrives. Will also choose husband when she finish college. Please hurry. Or you and Gurpal come here. Please do so now.

Your wife
Pali

He read the letter and put it behind the till to think about it. So after all this time she wanted to come home, or for him to go there, and thanks to Gurpal. He was pleased for the girl at least. He supposed that Pali had fallen out with her sister or been shamed by Gurpal's calls and unbetrothed status. He hadn't even known that Gurpal had been phoning. £400. No problem. Perhaps they should go out and join her, it would be good for him and Gurpal to get away, see family, for Gurpal to see India again. Could he leave the shop with the boys? Would he have anything to come back to?

'Time passes,' he thought, 'Time passes, and nothing really changes.'

The *News*es arrived with a thump on the counter, leaflets

falling out of them: A GREAT FAMILY DAY OUT AT THE NEW FOREST HAWK CONSERVANCY CENTRE. That must be the new place Paul was working at, that they were moving to. He'd seen the 'To Let' sign outside the café and Lucy had told him that they were moving to Paul's nature place. Paul had explained to him once about how they caught birds in a big net and ringed them.

'Euch! Who'd wanna work there?' Gurpal said when he told her. 'Hawks. Gross.' Her nostrils flared in disgust and she looked not unlike a golden eagle, standing on a rabbit, tearing it apart.

But it gave him a good idea. The next day he had a big order of chicken to prepare. He kept the heads, feet, some bones and entrails, and wrapped them up for Paul to give to his birds. There was nobody in when he went round to the café, so he left the bag on the doorstep with a note.

'For the new job. Good luck. John Vir.'

Two hours later there was Paul waving a dripping bin liner at him, slapping it down on the counter.

'What's this for? Don't you know Lucy's a vegetarian? She threw up everywhere. She's still crying and being upset, seeing something like this could be dangerous in her condition! Why did you leave this disgusting health hazard on our doorstep? Is it some kind of a sick joke? Because it's not funny. I'm thinking of calling the police. Don't you ever come near us again!'

'Hey, hang on, mate! It was just for your hawks. Help you in the new job.' He put the bag into a couple of very large Happy Shopper ones. 'Only trying to be neighbourly. Saw your leaflet,' he indicated the one he'd put behind the till to show Gurpal. 'Thought you'd like some bits for the birds.'

'Hawks? It's a Badger Centre, you arsehole!' And he left.

John Vir knew that he had finally fluffed it. That he had lost her for ever. There was no hope for him. He was a game-show contestant who makes it to the big money question, the car or £20,000 final, he has all the letters but he can't solve the last simple puzzle. The audience are yelling the answer, but he can't hear them. His minutes tick away and he's going home empty-handed. It was all up for John Vir.

44

M avis bought a pad of Forever Friends notepaper invites. Huge-headed rabbits and teddies announced the nuptials in shades of peach, grey and lemon. The ceremony was to be at 2.45 p.m. on 17 September at Southampton Registry Office and afterwards at the Bluebird Café. Mavis wasn't sure about the afterwards, the café. She thought that funny people went there, but Gilbert had wanted it there, and the price was certainly all right.

'Paul and Lucy would be upset if we didn't. They might be thinking I don't have time for them any more now I'm with you,' Gilbert told her.

'Well, you don't. And not with the wedding,' Mavis replied. She was right. Gilbert's days no longer stretched empty, identical, drip, drip, drip. After the bins there was shopping to do with Mavis and looking in catalogues for things, the new budgie to look after, and dinner and washing up, and trying to fix things, and the telly together, and supper and bed. Once he was in that warm flat with the door shut and Kenny turned up loud while Mavis got his dinner, the time just went. He hardly had time for any of his old stuff now.

'They're closing down. Moving to the Common,' he told her, hoping to elicit some sympathy for his old friends.

'I'm not surprised,' Mavis said. 'Funny ones go in there. Tree protesters and students. Not that I'm against trees, really. But all those funny teas and no meat.' She looked quite fierce. Until then Gilbert hadn't noticed how long her canines were.

'I'm taking some meat and no arguing. We can't have a wedding and no meat. Chicken and ham and that's final.'

'I don't know if Lucy will like that,' said Gilbert faintly.

'Well, she'll have to lump it then. We're paying and we take our own booze so what's the difference?'

Lucy and Paul were doing a finger buffet at £1.50 a head for twenty guests.

Crisps
Canapés
Pickles
Bridge rolls – egg and cress
              – cheese and pickle
Pizza slices
Mini quiches
Mini stuffed pancakes

'And peanuts,' Gilbert had told them, 'and Hula Hoops.' Lucy had put iced gems on the list too. And a peach ice cream she'd recently been experimenting with, with heart-shaped wafers; that could be on the house.

Mavis had ordered a cake from Bignells, the bakers. Just ten inches, sponge not fruit, no tiers. They'd been surprised and pretty impressed. It made a change from day-old bread and lardy cake.

'For your daughter, is it?' the girl had asked. 'I didn't know you had any kids.'

'No – me! Me and my Gilbert!'

'Isn't that nice. Been together long?'

'About six months.'

'Quick work! Congratulations!'

Mavis chose some embracing penguins and yellow ribbons for the top.

'That'll match my dress,' she had said.

'What, penguins? Nice!'

She had a yellow dress with black-and-white stripes, and a white bouclé (or bobbly) jacket and was planning to get some new shoes.

'I'm not so keen on wedding hats,' she told Gilbert. 'Do you mind?'

'You'll look lovely,' said Gilbert, on the softest wings, the thought was there. 'Just like my mum.'

FOR SALE OR TO LET
CAFÉ/SHOP PREMISES WITH FIRST-FLOOR FLAT

Cllr Doon had plans. A drop-in centre for the local community. Advice, help with filling out forms, an office base for community projects (there must be some around here). It was either that or it could go for more social housing. The housing associations were buying up everything around there. It ensured the properties were kept up. Nobody would expect the Bluebird to be turned into a real business, not a going concern, anyway.

Paul and Lucy had everything packed upstairs; books, clothes, kitchen stuff. Paul was going to borrow the van from the Badger Centre. Lucy hoped that it wouldn't be full of cobwebs and woodlice, or worse.

45

G ilbert was walking along the path beside the river from
Northam to St Denys in the shadows of the Meridian TV
Studios. The Itchen was going out. He was hoping to find a
wallet on the shore or to see some interesting birds. The mud
beneath the imported pebbles glittered green in the sun. The
university crew sculled by, hotly pursued by three swans.

'Row! Row! Go, swans, go!' yelled Gilbert. If you saw him
now in his Caramac jacket, all alone, wearing his baseball cap,
you'd know that he was on the edge. In Southampton they give
baseball caps out at the Department of Psychiatry.

'Here's your pills and here's your cap.' Choose between black
Coca-Cola ones, and ones from places you'll never make it to –
Florida, Hollywood, LA, NYC – you don't need to buy one,
they're standard issue for the mentally ill and people with
learning difficulties, the poor, the halt and the lame.

'A swan can break a man's arm with one beat of its wing,'
Gilbert cautioned himself.

The so-called Sprinter, the train from Portsmouth Harbour
to Cardiff, limped past on the track just a few yards from the
water's edge.

'It'll be doing that underwater soon,' he thought, as its fat
behind disappeared. 'It'll soon be on the wrong side of the
tracks, laughing on the other side of its face.'

He had been given his notice. It had come out of the blue to
him; everybody else had seen it coming. Mavis said he would be

all right with her though, and the council were going to try to find him another job. He was on the At Risk Register. He had some sandwiches that Mavis had given him crammed into his pocket. Cheese and piccalilli, his favourite.

He'd even had to help do himself out of a job, helping with the deliveries. There were no more council-issue bin bags now.

They came at dawn, crouching on trucks. At the signal they were off the back and down the road in formation. People sprang out of bed at the strange rumblings, threw back the nets to see them massing on the pavements and then spread out, one to each house. There were a few conscientious objectors. Some people found them ugly and didn't want them cluttering up the pretty Victorian terraces.

'Paul, quick! It's the wheelie bins!' Lucy shouted.

46

W hen Paul collected the boxes of samosas on the morning of the wedding he'd expected to see John Vir, had thought that he'd apologise for flying off the handle; but only Gurpal was there.

'Where's your dad?'

'Cash and Carry with my mum. You having a party?'

'Yes, it's our wedding,' Paul told her.

'That all you're having? Not many guests. We'll have two thousand samosas at my wedding.'

'Mmm,' said Paul. 'It's just a little party, but if you and your mum and dad want to drop in . . . It's at Bluebell Cottage on the Common, near the duck pond. This afternoon, after three.'

'Where they have the fair, you mean?'

'Yeah, quite near there. I'll draw you a map.' Paul drew a sketchy little map with directions on a brown paper bag. 'X marks the spot,' he said.

'I'll tell them,' said Gurpal.

And John Vir would have been pleased if she'd remembered to, if she hadn't used the bag with the map for the next customer.

The Brookeses and the Clouds were together at last. Lucy and Paul couldn't keep them apart any longer. There were no potential homes to look over, but they could still offer advice on pension plans and savings for the baby. ISAs vs. Baby Bonds.

Maggie Cloud and Jane Brookes were engaged in a secret guerilla war. Who would be favourite granny? There were also names to be discussed.

Paul and Lucy hit on the clever plan of only making public the most preposterous suggestions (Teague, for instance), so that when the real candidates were announced they would be gratefully accepted without criticism.

The Clouds and the Brookeses spent the night before the wedding at the Dolphin Hotel, grand for Southampton, and near the registry office. They met, by accident, in the lift on the way to breakfast, and had to sit together. The women agreed over their fresh fruit salad and natural yoghurt that the Dolphin would have been a jolly good venue for the wedding reception; but of course Lucy and Paul's simple DIY plans to hold it at Bluebell Cottage were very charming. The men had Full English Breakfast, and did nothing but grunt.

Meanwhile, at Bluebell Cottage everything was ready. With the restlessness of pregnancy, Lucy had it all finished by 8 a.m. She had put Paul in charge of drinks and moving furniture. He had just popped down to the Badger Centre, a few hundred yards across the Common, to borrow a few more chairs and quickly check some newts. Lucy was lying on the bed, sobbing.

Abigail and Teague parked their ancient Saab under the trees in Cemetery Road, and set off for Bluebell Cottage carrying presents, two bottles of champagne, a Le Creuset casserole and a brass door knocker of a badger.

The wedding invitations with the injunction 'No presents – but please bring a bottle' meant that people brought loads of champagne *and* presents, and Lucy and Paul acquired more stuff than many couples with very long wedding lists at John

Lewis. The whole process could be repeated in a few months for the baby shower.

They spotted Paul unlocking the Badger Centre gates. Teague stayed to help him carry the chairs and gave him a nip of brandy. Paul checked the display hive too. All was well.

Abigail knocked on the cottage door, feeling like someone with a walk-on part in a fairy story. Eventually, Lucy opened the door, her face as pink and puffy as a marshmallow. Tears and progesterone.

'Lucy! What's wrong?'

'I don't know.'

'Don't you want to marry him?'

'Yes. I don't know.'

'Well, you don't really have to.'

'But I want to.'

'Don't cry. Oh, I suppose you have to cry. Have a drink. Are you allowed?'

'One wouldn't hurt. But I don't want one. A cup of tea . . .'

Abigail hugged her and put the kettle on. 'Remember those Quiet Life tablets we took all through finals? I could go and get you some? But you'd better get ready, you've only got an hour and a quarter. Show me your dress!'

Lucy hadn't told Paul of her reservations about the text of the civil wedding ceremony. 'I know not of any reason why I should not be joined with A in matrimony.' Something like that. And then: 'I, B, take you, A, to be my husband.' It sounded to Lucy the same as 'Might as well then'. She could imagine it being part of a 'What are you driving now?' conversation between men at the reception. 'Well, gets you from A to B, and that's all you need.' Perhaps they should have done some research into alternative wedding services, scripts and venues.

The knot was tied, the confetti thrown. It was everybody back to Bluebell Cottage.

'Well, that went with a hitch!' Lucy joked to all the guests. Everyone loved her dress. In the photos she would look like a sepia tint against a line-up of classic navy blue outfits. During the ceremony she had felt the baby moving, a little fish flipping over and over.

Abigail was filling up people's glasses. The foil was off the food. Lucy had made blackberry ice cream and dozens of tiny little pies, and lots of pretty, fragrant things to eat. Everybody was happy. Paul headed for the kitchen for more drinks.

'Champagne and ginger beer!' Lucy called after him.

The ginger beer was ready for the wedding. The bottles had stood on the cool stone floor for three weeks. No one had touched them, and when Paul picked one up, went to tuck it under his arm and reach for another one, it exploded. Glass cut the air, smashing into another bottle and another bottle. A flying stopper hit Paul on the temple and he fell back against the door and down the step, arms up, legs stretched out. And that is how they found him. An X.

Lucy stroked his hair. His head was in her lap. Fennel sat at his feet.

'Paul, Paul,' Lucy said softly, as she tried to bring him round.

'Let me at him! I was in the League of Friends!' Mavis elbowed her way through the concerned guests. 'He's out cold,' she told them. 'I'd better give him the kiss of life.'

'No thanks, he's still breathing,' Lucy said quickly.

'This'll help then,' Mavis countered. She tipped her glass of champagne over Paul's forehead and on to Lucy's dress. 'Don't like the stuff much. Bubbles get up my nose. Repeats on me.'

'He might need an ambulance,' said Lucy. (Was this really her wedding?) But the bubbles had got up Paul's nose, and he spluttered and choked himself awake. 'Get a cloth please, someone.'

One fluttered before her and she wiped some of the stickiness away.

'Velvet does get the most unshiftable watermarks,' Soo Sholing told her. 'You'll need a jolly good dry-cleaner to restore that pile. I wonder if a silk dupion would have shown it.'

'Ease of stain removal wasn't really top of my list when I was choosing it,' said Lucy.

'Pity.'

Abigail and Maggie Cloud (reassured that her son was out of danger) swept up the broken glass and wiped ginger beer from the pantry walls and floor.

'I think they were about to paint in here anyway,' said Abigail. 'No need to bother with the ceiling.'

Maggie rolled her eyes at the ceiling. It was certainly in need of redecoration and more than a little cobwebby in places.

'Who is that woman who ruined Lucy's dress?' Maggie asked.

'Oh, Mavis.'

'Is she one of Lucy's relatives?' Maggie Cloud was very concerned. Would this person now be a fixture at family gatherings, have constant access to her grandchild?

'I don't know why she's here really,' said Abigail. 'She probably wasn't invited. Or she's to do with the Badger Centre now. I think it might have been open invitation to all of Paul's volunteers or something . . .'

James Cloud had helped his son to one of the beechwood steamer chairs that had arrived as wedding presents. Paul reclined, flanked by relatives, telling everyone that he was fine, although he did feel very odd and very embarrassed. He wasn't aware that feeling slightly stunned was a normal reaction to getting married. He lay blinking in the sunshine. Lucy was holding his hand with uncharacteristic devotion.

'I've got to go, Lucy, Paul, hope you feel better. I've got some copy to file for tomorrow. Hope you won't mind, just a little piece.' Soo Sholing kissed the air near them. 'Lovely wedding.'

'Won't you stay for some cake?' Lucy asked. Soo Sholing had forgotten that you were meant to stay at least for the cake. 'Never mind. We'll save you a bit.' She would also miss Lucy forgetting to throw her bouquet.

Soo Sholing picked her way across the garden, hoping that she wouldn't get too much mud on her new ankle-strap shoes. She had never been one for 'outdoors'. She was soon on the path back to the car park where she rang the newsdesk on her mobile. It was hardly front-page stuff, but a nice little story all the same.

'When are you doing the cake?' Lucy's mother asked. 'You don't want people to start going before you do it.'

'Now, I guess,' said Lucy. 'If Paul feels up to it.'

'Oh, I can cut it,' said Paul.

'And I would like a quiet word,' Jane Brookes added.

'It's a bit late for wedding night advice, don't you think?' joked James Cloud, rather lewdly, Lucy thought.

'It's not that,' Jane Brookes said, as she slipped her arm

around her daughter's shoulders and they walked towards the back door. 'I am so proud and pleased for you. It's lovely here. I was just wondering. That Mavis person who poured champagne all over you, she isn't one of Paul's aunts or something, is she? Surely she isn't a relative?'

'Just Badger Centre,' said Lucy. 'Don't worry.'

The rest of the Badger Centre volunteers, the committee and Cllr Doon had spent the reception sitting outside on some groundsheets, which they must have brought along themselves. Gilbert was with them, steadily eating. They were taking it in turns to go foraging in the kitchen for more food and drink. Lucy's teas would go like hot cakes at the Badger Centre.

At last the wedding cake was carried out and cut to muted cheers and applause and cries of 'Speech! Speech!'

'Just thank you all so much for coming and helping to make our day so happy,' said Lucy. She turned to Paul, but he didn't want to add anything.

It began to get dusky and cold. Abigail and Teague lit citronella garden flares and stuck them in the flower beds.

'Bit dangerous, that,' said Mavis. 'Come on, Gilb, time to go. You going our way as usual?' she asked Cllr Doon.

'Pleased to, my dears,' was the kind reply. The ribbon of guests, of hats and bags, and some half-empty bottles began to unfurl across the Common.

Abigail and Teague went round the garden with binbags while the Brookeses and Clouds loaded the dishwasher.

'Glad they saved this from the café,' said Jane. 'I wish I'd had one when Lucy was a baby.'

Lucy and Paul sat under the stars in the new chairs. The *News* was going to print.

BRIDEGROOM CHEATS DEATH
IN WEDDING DRAMA

Southampton bridegroom and father-to-be Paul Cloud had a lucky escape at his own wedding reception when he was knocked unconscious by flying ginger beer bottles. The celebrations almost came to an abrupt end when some bottles of the non-alcoholic, home-made drink exploded.

Soo Sholing, our Women's Page Editor, who was a guest at the wedding reception, said: 'Paul, who is manager of the Badger Centre, the city's flagship nature reserve, had just married Lucy Brookes, who writes a cookery column for my page. The party was in full swing when Paul went to fetch some more drinks.

'The next thing we knew was a few big bangs. I thought it was fireworks going off at first. We all rushed into the kitchen.

'There he was, knocked out, with some cuts from flying glass. He's making a good recovery.

'It could have been a lot worse really.'

A NOTE ON THE AUTHOR

Rebecca Smith was born in London in 1966. She lives in Southampton with her husband and three children, and is working on her second novel.

A NOTE ON THE TYPE

This old style face is named after the French-man Robert Granjon, a sixteenth-century letter cutter whose italic types have often been used with the romans of Claude Garamond. The origins of this face, like those of Garamond, lie in the late fifteenth-century types used by Aldus Manutius in Italy. A good face for setting text in books, magazines and periodicals.